The Delecroie Curse

By:
Teresa M. Sanders

PublishAmerica
Baltimore

First printing

ISBN: 1-4137-8962-5
PUBLISHED BY PUBLISHAMERICA, LLLP
www.publishamerica.com
Baltimore

Printed in the United States of America

June -
life is what you make of it. Have fun! with no worries

I dedicate this book to all of my friends and family members who have given me support and motivation throughout everything: my parents, Mike & Debi; my friends Alexis & Pete Gillespie, Barb & Gary Michaels, and Hope; and also my siblings, my niece Corrine, and my nephew Bradley.

Chapter One

I walked out of the school and smiled. I had officially completed the sixth grade; next year I would be in the middle school! Now my summer vacation was to begin, three months of doing nothing but relaxing and enjoying my time doing nothing. Kari, my best friend, was rambling on next to me about how she did not want to spend her summer at her grandparents' farm in North Dakota. I, however, was excited. My mom had decided that she would take Sam and me on an all-girls trip up to San Francisco, and we were leaving first thing tomorrow! She had even splurged and bought us all plane tickets! So we won't even have to make the three-hour drive!

"Tanya, Sam is waiting, and she does not look too happy."

I glanced at the corner and saw my older sister looking just as Kari said: not happy. Sam and I were pretty close; we were actually only 10 months apart. Mom and Dad could not have any children, and they had wanted some very badly, so they had looked into adoption at two different agencies. The first had placed Sam with them; she had been two years old. Then the second agency had called and said they had a 14-month-old baby girl, and that had been me, Tanya Johnson.

"Sam, what is wrong?"

"Mom is going to freak; I am going to be grounded for the entire summer."

"What happened?"

She handed me a folded piece of paper; I unfolded it and looked down at her report card.

"Sam, at least you could tell Mom that since it is only a D, you do not have to retake the class."

"You know what she said. Math is just not my subject, unlike you, whom everything just comes to."

"We will figure something out, I promise. By next week, Mom will have forgotten all about the grade."

We got to our neighborhood and said goodbye to Kari. "Do not get too lost on the farm! It will only be three months."

"Yeah, maybe next year I can talk my parents into summer school in Switzerland!"

"We will write!"

Sam and I waved goodbye and then walked across the yard to our house.

"Hi, girls! How was your last day of school?"

"Great! We got our schedules for seventh grade, and Kari and I have most of our classes together!"

"That is great! Sam, how was yours?"

"Good."

"Care to expand?"

"I went, it was good, I came home."

"All right, how about your report cards then?"

I handed mine over, as did Sam. She looked over them and then at us.

"Tanya, you did very well, but please go up to your room."

I looked at Sam and gave her my "I am sorry" face and quickly left the room. Our house was quite small—two bedrooms, a bath, kitchen, and living room. So whenever one of us got into trouble, the other always got sent to our room.

Twenty minutes later, Sam came into our room. I looked up from my desk at her. "Well?"

"I am grounded for two weeks after we get back from San Fran, and then I will have a tutor to recover the algebra book, so I will be up to date at the beginning of next year."

"What are we sacrificing for your tutor?"

"My softball. You are in the clear; my failing a class should not disrupt your chosen activity."

"I am sorry; I will play catch with you all summer."

Since Sam was stuck in our bedroom all night, I stayed with her playing games. I went to the kitchen to get a snack and overheard Mom and Dad in their bedroom.

"She is four years old and just adorable."

"I know, but we do not have any room; we will have to move. We cannot expect the girls to share their already cramped room with a four-year-old."

"I thought about that. The girls would have to go to a community college for the first two years; Tanya will probably get a scholarship anyways. And no more big vacations, only weekend trips every once in a while. There is a three-bedroom-two-bath, three streets over; it needs some work, but we can do it."

"Let's do it. I will tell the girls while we are in San Francisco if you could make the arrangements. That house is vacant, so I am sure we could move right in."

"I already talked to the bank; they said yes, so I could have us all moved in by the time you guys get back next week."

"Great! When can we get Bella?"

"Two weeks. We may be able to bring her home in a week if everything goes well."

"Good, I will tell the girls."

I turned around and went back to my room and shut the door.

"Sam, you won't believe what they are going to do."

"Tanya, you are red."

"While we are in SF, Dad is going to move us over to that house on Bird, and then they are adopting another child."

"Calm down, what are you talking about?"

"I am talking about them. I overheard them talking, and they are going to adopt a four-year-old named Bella, and Dad has made all the arrangements to move us over to that house on Bird, and it will be all done by the time we get back."

"What were they going to do, just act like nothing has happened until we get back?"

"Mom said that she would take care of telling the girls on our trip."

"Yeah right, what happened to being a family and making family decisions?"

"Who knows?"

Sam and I said no more than we had to during the flight or on the ride to the hotel. After we got to our room, Mom turned to us.

"All right, I have had enough. I am planning on having a fun vacation with my daughters, and you two are acting like spoiled brats. What is going on?"

"We know what you are doing."

"What?"

"We know, and you did not even tell us."

"You know what?"

"The house, and the girl."

"Oh."

"Tanya overheard you last night."

I shot Sam a look.

"Well, Tanya, we will discuss your eavesdropping and consequences later; however, you are correct. We were not sure what we were going to do, so please, just listen. It all happened very fast. Bella's only parent was just arrested and sentenced to a very long time in prison. An associate of your father brought her to our attention; we could not leave this little girl on her own. Our house is not big enough for all of us, so we are going to move. I was going to tell you two tonight."

"So we still have to share a room?"

"Yes."

"Can't Tanya share will Bella?"

"Hey!"

With that, we started out on our vacation. We went shopping, on a boat ride, to some very cool restaurants, and everywhere else we could imagine. On our final night, Mom decided that we would go to a show. We each even got a new outfit to wear! Mom was enjoying it; however, Sam and I were bored. A little after intermission, I came up with an excuse that I had to go use the restroom. I decided to use the one in the lower lobby to take up more time. Sam was behind me; we were chasing each other. I ran around the corner and right into a very pretty lady.

"Sara, what are…?"

"I am sorry, ma'am, my sister and I were playing around, and it got out of hand."

She was starring at me, and then responded, "That is all right, Tanya."

"Hey, how did you know my name?"

She looked around. "I heard your sister call you that. Do you girls need any help with anything?"

"No, thank you. Our Mom is probably wondering where we are; we should get back to our seats."

The lady seemed a little flustered and then agreed.

We arrived home to our new house. Sam and I were happy; Dad had actually listened and had our room painted lavender and blue. The house was nice. The room for Bella was painted pink and had her name in block letters along the wall and was full of stuffed animals. She was due to arrive in eight days, and we were starting to look forward to it, although we did not have much to do since we were both grounded—Sam for her grades and me for my eavesdropping.

Chapter Two

We had been in our new home for five days. Sam and I were just starting the unpacking of our boxes and setting up our room. When we sat down to lunch, the doorbell rang. I got up to answer it. There were two police officers along with some people in suits.

"Young lady, we need to speak with your parents."

Mom was behind me. "Officer, what is wrong?"

"We are here on behalf of Craig and Kerstin Delecroie regarding the wellbeing of Miss Tanya Alexandra Delecroie."

"All right, but what does that have to do with us?"

"You are in possession of their missing daughter."

"No, we have our two children whom we have legally adopted."

The officer looked at me. "This child standing next to you was never legally placed up for adoption. She is the youngest daughter of the Delecroies, and they would like her back."

"Mom, what are they saying?"

"Tanya, hush. How on earth can you say that?"

The officer held out two photos to Mom, she took them, and then her jaw dropped. I looked over at what she was holding. The first one was of three babies, about one year old, identical except for the colors they were wearing. The second was a picture of two girls in school uniforms; the only thing was they looked exactly like me. Identical.

"We are here to return the child to her parents."

I grabbed my mom's arm. "Mommy."

She put her arm around me. "She is not going anywhere, and I am going inside to call my attorney."

"That is fine, ma'am; however, said child must stay here. She is now in the custody of the state until this situation is resolved."

"Well, officer, she is staying with me. You may come into my house as long as you do not try to take her without her consent."

"That is fine, for now." The officers and the people in suits all entered our house, Mom and I walked into the kitchen, and one of the ladies followed us.

"Mom, make them go away."

"I am sorry, ladies. Someone must have Tanya in sight at all times to ensure that you do not try and take off with her again."

"We did not take off with her, we adopted her. Sam, please go tell your father that I need him in here and also ask him to get out the adoption papers for Tanya." She quickly turned and left the room without asking any questions. Mom called the attorney, and by the time she hung up, Dad was in the room with Sam right behind.

"What is going on?"

Mom looked at me and then at the lady. "May the girls go to their room? It is on the second floor, the stairs are right there, and you can see if they leave it."

"I guess that would be all right; however, you and your husband must stay down here."

"Girls, go on,"

Sam and I went up the stairs and both sat down next to the door. Trying to hear everything that was being said. It seemed to take forever. Two hours later, Mom and Dad's lawyer showed up, and we heard them talking.

"Jeff, Liz, listen. They have done the research; it is all right here. All the time is linked. She is identical to the other two, they have the same name, and you adopted her two weeks after their daughter was kidnapped. We have no argument; the only thing that would happen is she would be put into protective custody. They have the best attorneys, and you will go bankrupt and still not hold a chance. They never put her up for adoption; she was kidnapped."

"So you are telling us to give up on our child?"

"She is twelve, and it will be tough for her, but they could hold this in courts for years. That entire time she would be living in a foster home with supervised visitation only. You can turn her over to them, and we can sue for visitations, weekends, holidays. It would be in her best interest."

"She is our little girl."

"She is also their little girl; they love her, and a foster home won't."

I was standing with the door open now, tears rolling down my face. Mom looked up and saw me. She also had tears rolling down her cheeks.

"We can get visitation?"

"Mom, NO!" I yelled.

"I cannot make any promises, but we can sue for it. She has grown up and knows you as her parents. A quick separation would not be good for her mental state."

"Then it is what we are going to have to do."

"Mommy, NOOOO! You can't do that! Daddy, tell her that you can't do that!" I screamed, running down the stairs.

"I am sorry, sweetie, but they are right, these people love you. I cannot see you in a foster family for who knows how long? We love you, and this is going to kill us." Mom had her arms around me and we were both crying.

"We can call the Delecroies and have them come here to get her, or we can take her and turn her over to them at the airport."

"I do not want her to travel in a police car."

"They are down the road, and I will have them come up and get her."

"Mommy, please don't let them take me."

"Sweetie, I am so sorry, but they are going to take you away. Would you rather go to a foster home for years while we fight this out?"

"At least you would be fighting."

"We are going to fight, just in another way, sweetie."

"Daddy, please!" I begged.

"We love you so very much, baby."

"The Delecroies are pulling into the driveway. There is no need for her to pack anything; her parents will provide her with everything she needs."

"MY stuff, I need my stuff," I cried out.

Mom wiped the tears from my eyes. "You need to be brave for us, and you will be treated well. If they don't treat you right, then all you have to do is call, and we will be there and have you out of there in no time. Sam," she said, turning to my sister, "could you please go up and get your sister's personal things, put them into a bag, and bring it down?"

The doorbell rang, and one of the men in suits went to open it. I glanced over to see a man and woman enter; then I froze. The lady was the same one that I had run into in the theater in San Francisco. He was dressed in a suit, and she was in a skirt and blouse.

"Tanya, this is Kerstin and Craig Delecroie, and this is Tanya." The lady came over and gave me a hug. I stood there.

"I have missed you so much." She let me go and looked at me.

"Kerstin, we need to get going, so why don't we let Tanya say her goodbyes?"

I just stared at him, and then I felt her hand on my shoulder. "He is right, please say your goodbyes."

I turned back into my mom's arms and started crying again.

"Remember what I said, sweetie." Dad came over and put his arms around me also. "Just remember we will always love you. You are still our little girl."

I wiped my eyes off. "I will."

"Ready to go, Tanya?"

I ran over and gave Sam a hug.

"I love you, tell Kari what happened, and I will call you as soon as I can. You are my best friend and my sister." Kerstin walked over and put her arm around me; she gently led me toward the door.

When we got to the entrance, I stopped, turned around, and looked at everyone. One of the officers was holding my bag and my trumpet. Kerstin dropped her arm and slid her hand over mine and then led me out of the door. I did not realize that I was still crying. Craig was waiting, holding the car door open; I got in and looked out of the window. Kerstin sat next to me in the back, and Craig drove. I did not say anything, and they took after my lead. After a little while in silence, I noticed we were entering a side entrance of the airport. "Where are we going?"

"We are taking you home, baby. We live outside of Los Angeles."

"What? No one told me we were going to be so far away."

"Well, that is where we spend most of our time. Do you have any questions you want to talk about?"

"No."

"All right, we will talk later."

The car pulled up to a small plane; then a man came around and opened my door. "The plane is ready for departure whenever you are, sir," the man said to Craig as he walked around the car.

"Good, Tanya has a few things in the trunk."

"Yes, sir."

I stood looking at the plane and then felt another hand on my shoulder. The tail of the plane was painted with *Delecroie International*. "This is yours?" I mumbled.

Kerstin looked down at me. "Yes, this is one of ours." I followed her onto the plane. The front section had a couch and a table with chairs. I sat in a chair and looked out the window. Kerstin sat down next to me and handed me a tissue; I was still crying. I stared out the window during the entire flight.

When we landed, there was a limo waiting outside of the plane. After driving for a while, we came to a place that looked like a castle. It was surrounded by a twelve-foot wall and cast-iron gate at the entrance.

"Welcome home, Tanya, back to Delecroie Manor."

I did not say anything, but exited the car and looked at the marble steps. Kerstin once again put her arm around me and led me up the stairs into the house. Inside the house in the entranceway stood three young women.

"Tanya, I would like you to meet your sisters. Kate, she is 25, Ann is 23, and Elizabeth is 15."

I smiled shyly at them, but my face must have shown how I was confused.

"Hope and Sara are at school; they will be done next weekend. I think we will surprise them."

"School? It is Saturday."

"Yes, they go to boarding school in Connecticut."

"Oh."

"Why don't I show you your room and then give you a tour of the house? Then we will have dinner. You can explore the grounds this week."

"I am not hungry."

"That is all right."

I followed her up the stairs.

She explained how my room was to be in the west wing on the second floor, along with Hope and Sara's—their room was in the east wing; Kate, Elizabeth, and Ann were on the third floor in the west wing. The pool, theater, and tennis courts were the first floor east wing, and the living areas, dining room, and offices were the first floor west wing. Guests stayed in the east wing on the third floor. My room was the fourth one on the left. Kerstin opened the double doors, and I was shocked. The room was bigger than my entire house. There was a large, king-size canopy bed. The canopy, carpets, curtains, and linens were all in dark lavender. There was also a couch and an entertainment center, along with a desk and a fully loaded computer.

"If you do not like the color, we can have it changed."

"I like purple."

"I hoped you still did."

"What?"

"When you were babies, we color coded things so we knew what belonged to whom; your color was yellow. One day you started screaming and threw everything yellow; you took off what you could of your outfits and would not stop screaming. Then you grabbed Elizabeth's purple blanket and would not settle down after she let you have it. We then changed your color to purple so we could be through with the tantrums."

"Oh." I walked into the room and looked around. On the dresser was a picture of three toddlers, one in pink, one in peach, and the third in purple. I realized looking at the picture that my nightmare was not going to be ending; however, I did feel connected to these two other girls who looked like me. Why, I am not sure.

"That picture was taken a week before you disappeared."

"How did it happen?"

"I am not sure really."

"Any mother who cares would not just lose a child."

"Tanya, I care more about you than anything."

"Obviously not. My mom and dad always knew where I was or what I was doing."

"I was at the park with you, Hope, Sara, and Kate. The nanny had taken Ann and Elizabeth to some play dates. Kate was thirteen; she was playing on the jungle gym and fell. She was screaming, I ran over to her, she had broken her arm, I picked her up, and ran her to the car. When I returned to get you three, you were gone. I was not more than twenty feet away the entire time. I searched; nobody saw anything. I am so sorry."

"I have had a wonderful life, my parents love me, and I love them."

"I am glad that such loving people raised you. Your father and I are grateful to them, and now we have out baby girl back."

"I am their little girl, not yours."

"You have always been my baby, my little girl, and you always will be no matter where you are."

I set the picture down and walked over to the window and stared out. After a moment, I felt her hand brush the back of my hair. "You have a good view of the stables from here. Do you ride?"

"No."

"Well then, we will have to get you some lessons. To the left are the outdoor tennis courts and pools. The rackets are in the pool house."

"I do not play."

"Well, we can get you lessons for that too."

"I do not want them."

"Well, give it some time."

"Whatever."

"Well, you probably want to settle in, so I will go see if supper is about ready. Your closet is full of clothes. I will be back in just a little while." She gave me a hug and walked out. The first thing I did was look around for a phone. It was sitting on the desk; I picked it up and dialed home.

"Hello?"

"Mom?"

"Tanya, honey, how are you? Do they know you called?"

"No. I miss you."

"We miss you too."

"I want to come home."

"Baby, I want you here too, but you have to give this a chance, and we are going to the court on Monday to ask for visitation."

"They have several other kids. Why they have to have me here, I am not sure."

"Because if someone had kidnapped you or Sam from us, we would do anything to find you and bring you home. They are just doing the same thing."

"Mom, it is just not the same…Uh-oh." Kerstin had walked back into the room. "I gotta go. I love you, Mom." I hung up the phone.

"Tanya, how are the Johnsons?"

"All right."

"When I dropped Hope and Sara off last year at boarding school, they called me every day for the first month."

"So you are not mad? I can call them?"

"As long as it does not come between you giving us a chance. Supper is ready; would you like to change?"

"I like what I am wearing."

"All right, we are going down to the porch."

They were all staring at me when I entered. I took a seat next to Elizabeth, and then Kerstin sat down next to me. "I cannot believe how much you look like the twins."

"Elizabeth, you are aware that they are triplets. Hope and Sara are not twins, nor do we refer to them as such."

"Yes, sir, I am sorry."

"Tanya, do you play any sports?"

"I like soccer and also ice-skating."

"Oh good! Dad, the ice rink may get used again!"

"Ice rink?"

"Yes, when Ann was seven, Dad took her to the Olympics, and when they got back, she wanted to be a skater, so Dad had a rink installed. She quit six months later."

"Thanks for bringing up that again, Kate. Tanya, do you play any instruments?"

"I played the piano for a while, but now I play the trumpet."

"The trumpet is not a very appropriate instrument for a girl."

"Craig, please stop."

"Actually, in my band all the trumpet players were girls."

"How odd. Oh well, we will get you back into those piano lessons."

"No, thank you."

"Tanya, why don't you tell us some more about yourself, how you are as a student, what you like to do?"

"Well, I get all A's in school, I was on the school soccer team, I skated on weekends, and Sam and I would go roller-blading to the park, and Dad would always take us camping during the summer."

"Sounds like you have kept busy."

"My parents always encouraged us to keep busy with outside activities."

"Tanya, tomorrow night for dinner we will have some business associates here. Dinner will take place in the formal dining room. Your maid will set your dress out for you, and your mother or one of your sisters will help you with your hair. Please be ready by 5 p.m."

"I do not wear dresses."

"Well, you do now."

I just stared at him. *How dare he try to tell me what I will wear?*

"Tanya, I do not think that it will help if I try and baby you. You will be treated and expected to act as if you were raised in our house."

"But I wasn't." I stood up and walked back into the house.

"Craig, not now, give her some time," I heard Kerstin say. I headed back up the stairs and found my way back to the bedroom. I walked over to the bookshelves and found a baby book. I picked it up, sat down on the couch, and opened it:

Baby Book
Infant: Tanya Alexandra Delecroie
Born: September 5, 1988
Mother: Kerstin Alexandra Delecroie
Father: Craigory Thomas Delecroie III
Multiple Birth:
Born Third of Three Girls:
Hope Victoria
Sara Breanne
Tanya Alexandra

I flipped through the book; Kerstin had everything filled out until January 4th, 1990. That day had a newspaper article attached about the kidnaping. My first word had been "mommy," my first step had been at 10 months, and I had been the first of the triplets. Favorite food had been apples. I closed the book after the recordings had been finished.

"I did not know what else to put in there. I wanted to have filled it in until you were five."

"I did not know you came in."

"Sorry, I am not used to knocking for this room; I am not used to you being back in here."

"This was my room when I was a baby?"

"Yes, it was. For a while I did not let anyone change a thing about it. When I saw you last week, I was shocked. I thought you were Sara. She was with me in San Francisco for the weekend. Then I realized it was you; I could not believe it. I knew I would have you back. So I had the room redone so you would not come home to the nursery you left."

"My birthday is September 5th?"

"Yes. My, I did not even think about that. You would not know that, you were too young to know when it was."

"October 11th, that is what the adoption agency told my parents."

"Well, you are actually a month older then!"

"Great," I said sarcastically.

"Tanya, I was thinking. I know this is all very awkward for you. I think after you and your sisters see each other again, things will be a little easier for you, so I want to take you to Hartford. You can see your sisters and see their school."

"You took me away from my family and are going to send me to boarding school? Why didn't you just ask my parents for visits?" I was outraged.

"Calm down, you are not going to boarding school. You will live here and attend the same school that Elizabeth goes to. I cannot bring the girls home early because they are taking their exams now, and I thought you could see it so you would know what they are talking about when they refer to school."

"Do I have a choice?"

"Yes, you will always have a choice."

"Not so far. So will everyone be going out there?"

"No, your father has to go out of town for meetings, and Elizabeth has her exams also this week."

"Where does Elizabeth go to school?"

"St. Mary's School for Girls. We will leave on Monday morning; as for tomorrow, it will be pretty boring. After dinner, Ann will be called to the hospital for an emergency; however, it will be her boyfriend, Chris. Kate will have some big case files to go through for an appearance in court Monday morning, and Elizabeth will have to study for her exams."

"It sounds like this happens often."

"Yes, at least once a month or so. Do not be afraid to tell them that you are exhausted."

"Okay."

She walked over to the larger dresser and opened up the top drawer, pulling out a nightgown.

"It is getting late, and you have had a big day, so why don't you get ready for bed? Your father and I have to meet some people for drinks tonight, so I need to go get ready. I will be back in a little while. Please put this on." She laid the nightgown down on the bed, smiled at me, and then left. I walked over and looked at the silk, purple nightgown. It was nice but not me. I liked to wear a tee shirt and boxer shorts to bed. Besides, I was not tired; it was only 8 p.m. There were three doors off the room other than the main entrances. I opened the first, which led to a large bathroom, the second to a large closet filled with clothes, and the third to a small room that had three student desks and a chalkboard. This room had two other doors. One led into the hallway and the second to another room that looked exactly like mine except it was in pink. I looked around the other room. On the dresser was the same picture of the three babies I had on my dresser; this dresser also had a picture of two girls about eleven years old. They were both wearing white blouses and blue skirts, and each looked very happy.

"Tanya, here you are."

"Sorry, I was just…"

"You are allowed to explore. On the right is Hope. Sara is on the left."

"Whose room is this?"

"Hope's. Sara's is across the hall. Now let's get you back into your room and changed." She headed back through the room through which we had first entered.

"What is this room?"

"This is the classroom. Your father did not want them going to school so young, so he hired a teacher and transformed this into a classroom."

"But there are three desks."

"Yes, we were always ready for you to return."

"Oh."

She handed me the nightgown. "Go change, please."

"I normally wear tees and boxers to bed."

"I am sorry, I only have nightgowns here for you, and I will have to get some of the others for you."

I took it and then went to change. When I returned, she was sitting on the end of my bed. She got up and walked over to the vanity and picked up a brush. I am not sure why, but for some reason I actually felt safe with her. I followed her gesture for me to sit on the stool; she started to brush my hair.

"My mother used to brush my hair."

"Did you grow up here?"

"No, I grew up in Australia. My parents moved there when I was seven."

"Oh." When she was done brushing my hair, I crawled into the bed and did fall asleep before she left.

Chapter Three

The next morning, I woke up and prayed that my nightmare would be over. It was not. I was still in this strange place. I picked up the phone and decided to tell Kari myself. I had her number, and what did I care about the long distance? These people obviously had money. I dialed the number she left with me every summer.

"Hello, Mrs. Thomas. May I please speak with Kari?" There was a pause and then Kari answered.

"Hey! What is going on? I don't even get to watch TV here on the farm."

"Well, a lot has changed. Apparently my name is not Tanya Johnson."

"Quit being funny, you know you were adopted, so your name is Tanya Johnson."

"Nope, apparently I was never legally adopted because I was never put up for adoption."

"What are you rambling on about?"

"Yesterday the police showed up and took me away from my home. Oh yeah, my parents moved because they are adopting a four-year-old named Bella, but that's besides the point. Last week in SF, this lady was there with her daughter, and she spotted me. Apparently I am the youngest child and was kidnapped; then Mom and Dad adopted me, so the adoption was not legal. The lady tracked me down, got a court order to have me returned to them, and on top of it all, I am a triplet. My legal name is Tanya Alexandra Delecroie."

"You are getting pretty good at coming up with stories to make me think things are actually happening, but you are going a little overboard this time," she said, laughing.

"It is all true."

"Yeah, right."

Then there was a knock at the door, and the maid entered.

"Miss Tanya, you are awake. Your mother will be here shortly, and she asked that you will be dressed, and then she will take you on a tour of the grounds."

"Yes, Mary."

"Tanya, who was that? It did not sound like Sam."

"That was Mary, the maid. These people are loaded. In all legal purposes, I am the youngest biological daughter of Craig and Kerstin Delecroie."

"You are not kidding?"

"No, and my nightmare will not go away, Kari. Help me! I would rather be with you on the farm."

"I am sorry to here that, baby."

I turned my head and saw Kerstin standing in the doorway.

"Kari, I have to go. I will talk to you soon, I promise." I hung up the phone and turned back to Kerstin.

"I thought you were going to start knocking," I said coldly and stared right at her.

"You are right, I should have; however, I am hoping you will change your mind about us."

I sat on the edge of my bed and did not say anything. She walked into the closet and brought out a purple jumper with a white blouse. "Here, go change and then I will show you around the grounds."

"I want to wear shorts and a tee shirt."

"Your father does not approve of that type of outfit, and as he said last night, he is going to expect you to act and dress like you were raised in this house."

Rather than arguing, I changed and then followed her out the door. I did have fun for a little bit. In the stables I met the horses, and they took my mind off of being there, a little ironic if you think about it. I actually had my own horse. Then I went swimming in the pool, which was huge; Sam would have loved it. We ate lunch by the pool, and Elizabeth joined us. I returned to my room at 4 p.m., and Kerstin told me to start getting ready for the party; I decided to call home first.

"Tanya, I love you, sweetie, but should you be calling here? Do they know?"

"Do they know that I am on the phone right now, no. However, Kerstin said that I am allowed to call you as long as it does not disrupt my getting to know them."

"Good, I am glad. How are you doing?"

"All right. I went swimming in the pool today, and then I met my horse."

"You have a horse?"

"Yes, Buttercup. Hope and Sara named it."

"How are you getting along with your sisters? Is it weird to have two people around that look exactly like you?"

"I am not sure, I have not met them yet."

"Why not?"

"They are in Hartford; Kerstin is going to take me to meet them tomorrow."

"You are going across the country?"

"Yes, but we are not staying long. She wants me to get used to this house. The only reason we are going is because Hope and Sara are taking tests all week and cannot miss them. I guess."

"Well, at least they realize you need some stability."

"How is Sam? And what is going on with Bella?"

"Sam is all right; she misses you. I sent her to the mall with her friends; she did not want to leave. They dropped off Bella yesterday earlier than we expected her; it was a very busy day. She is probably just like you are right now: scared and in a strange place, but she will adjust, just as you will."

Kerstin knocked on my door, which was already open. When I looked up, she pointed at her watch.

"Mom, I have to go. I'm being called downstairs. I love you."

"Love you too, sweetie."

I hung up the phone and turned back to Kerstin.

"Sorry, baby. Here, why don't you go put this on?" she said, handing me a violet dress. I went into the bathroom and changed, then returned to the main room. She was sitting on the couch.

"Come here and I will do your hair."

I sat down next to her and allowed her to french braid my hair. When she was done, she took my hand, and we went to the dining room. Everyone was already in there.

"Ladies and gentlemen, I would like to present to you all my wife escorting my youngest daughter, Tanya Alexandra." I was now standing in a room of 30 people, and all eyes were on me. Not even realizing it, I found myself stepping closer to Kerstin for protection. I think it surprised her as much as it did me; however, she put her arm around me and held me close to her side.

"Do not be scared; they are not as bad as they look," she whispered into my ear.

"Well, Craig, it looks like she and your wife have adapted quickly."

"Yes, however, Joseph, they do say that a child will never forget the sound of their mother's voice."

Craig tried to take me around to meet all of his associates, but I refused to leave Kerstin's side. He was getting annoyed with me; however, she told him to leave me alone, that he was expecting too much from me. He was not happy, but he did as she asked. Elizabeth came over by us; she was tired of being asked, "Do you like having your sister back?" We eventually sat down to dinner; the conversation was very boring. As soon as dessert was served, Ann's pager went off, and she excused herself to go to the "hospital." Soon after, Kate and Elizabeth both left. I leaned over and asked Kerstin if I could be excused; however, Craig overheard and insisted that I stay no matter what Kerstin said to him. I was very tired from the day, and bored out of my mind. I fell asleep in my chair.

"I am going to take her upstairs now. I would have rather she fell asleep up there than down here, but it is too late now."

I opened my eyes and looked at Kerstin. She smiled at me and then helped me up.

"Come on; let's get you into bed." She walked me up to my room and then got out a fresh lavender nightgown and handed it to me. "Go change, baby."

When I came back into the room, Kerstin had turned down my bed, and she was standing next to the bookshelf, holding a children's book. I walked over and climbed into the bed; she sat down next to me.

"When your sisters were little, every night before bed they would crawl into one of their beds, and then I would read them a book. This was their favorite: *The Lost Princess*. They made me change the princess' name to Tanya."

"Did they remember me?"

"Yes, for weeks they would call your name. Hope would only fall asleep with your teddy bear."

"I do not remember anything."

"You were very young and had no one to remind you. I would have been very surprised if you had."

"Do you have to go back to the party?"

"No, your father will be so carried away he will never remember that I am gone. Tanya baby, I love you."

I smiled at her, but did not say anything. She bent over and kissed my forehead and then left the room, turning out the lights.

I was awakened in the morning by the maid and told to be down to breakfast in thirty minutes. She then set out and outfit and left the room. I got up and dressed, then went downstairs to breakfast. Ann was sitting at the table, so I sat next to her. Kerstin walked in shortly after.

"Good morning, girls. Elizabeth has already left for school; where is Kate?"

"Mom, she left with a suitcase and said something about eloping with William."

Kerstin looked at Ann and then quickly produced her cell phone. "Kate, where are you?...Well, you better turn around and come home right now...I do not care, we talked and we agreed...Kate Lynn, if I have to come there I will, but I was going to take Tanya to surprise Hope and Sara, so if you want to be the reason for ruining it...Thank you, we will see you shortly."

She hung up the phone and turned back to us. "Girls, I am telling you right now that I love you, but do not ever try to elope because the consequences are not going to be pretty."

"Mom, you used the triplets against her."

"Yes, I did, and I do not regret it. Nancy, please have Kate's bag packed to accompany Tanya and me to Hartford."

"Mom, you are making her go with you?"

"Yes, I cannot have her doing this while I am 2,000 miles away."

"What about her job?"

"If she was going to elope then she had the time off already. Why did you not come tell me when she left?"

"I can see where she is coming from."

"All she has to do is show up."

"Yes, however, she is the one in the media lime light. Elizabeth and I can hide behind her. She is the first heir, and you and Dad are always in the papers or magazines. Kate is now the one to get followed; Hope and Sara are still too young to be of much interest, and then you have Tanya."

"What about me?"

"You are the youngest and also the most famous."

"What?"

"Ann."

"Mom, she is. She is a household name. When you were born, you were the Delecroie Triplets, and everyone loves babies. Then your name and picture went national after you where kidnapped. And now with you being returned, the papers are buzzing again with the name Tanya Alexandra Delecroie."

"What?"

She opened her bag and pulled out a copy for the *New York Times*. My picture was on the front; the title "Rags to Riches" was next to it.

"You, little sister, are as famous as the President of the United States."

Kerstin had in the meantime left the room. I found her and Kate in the entranceway.

"Mother, why do I have to go with you?"

"To keep me company. Your sisters are going to be fully occupied."

"I do not want to go."

"Too bad, I want you to go."

"Mom, this is so unfair."

"End of discussion. Good, Tanya, you are here. Out to the car, both of you."

Kate fixed a glare on Kerstin, but she was ignored. Kerstin opened the door and gestured for us to exit.

"Mother, I am not going."

"Kate, should I start with the credit cards or your new car?"

Kate's glare went away and turned to a face of shock. "Mom!"

"Well."

"Fine," Kate stated and followed me out to the limo, a white one.

"How many limos do you have?"

"Four here, one in New York, and two in London."

"New York and London?"

"Yes, we have a penthouse in New York City, and an estate outside of London."

I watched a movie on the flight. When we arrived into Hartford, a limo met us. "You did not say that you had a limo here."

"We do not, this one is rented." Kerstin had decided that we would first go to the hotel and then proceed to the Buchanan Academy for Girls. The hotel was very fancy; Kerstin had reserved the presidential suite. There was a living room, dining room, four bedrooms, and five bathrooms.

The academy was about 15 minutes away, and it was very impressive. A ten-foot high brick wall covered in vines and a large gate at the entrance surrounded the perimeter. The drive was about five-hundred yards before there stood three large buildings that looked about 100 years old. The center building was larger than the other two.

"What do you think?"

"It is nice"

"Yes, it is. The central building is the main school building; the two side buildings are the apartments for the girls. On the other side is a large pond; beyond that are the horse stables and sports fields."

We walked into the main entrance. This school was unlike any school I had been to; it looked more like Delecroie Manor than a school. I followed Kerstin into what would be the den. It was the office. She held the door open for me. There was a lady sitting at a desk, and she looked up at me when I walked in.

"Good afternoon, Hope, hmm, Sara? I am sorry, I guess I am having trouble telling you apart. Which one are you?"

"Neither. I am Tanya."

Her jaw dropped as she looked at me; then I felt Kerstin's arm go around me.

"Maggie, I would like to introduce you to my youngest daughter, Tanya Alexandra."

"Wow, I read that you got her back, but to actually see her. Congratulations, Mrs. Delecroie."

"Thank you. Now, Hope and Sara have not heard the news, correct?"

"Yes, ma'am, they have no idea. I will let Mrs. Winterhaven know you are here."

"Thank you." The lady turned and walked away.

"We are going to have your sisters called in here, and then you can surprise them."

"It is 4:30 p.m. How late do they have classes?"

"Until 5:30. They have classes from 8 a.m. to 11:30 a.m., then from 2 p.m. to 5:30 p.m. They found that they pay attention better and succeed more often."

"That would suck."

"Watch your language."

"Ma'am, Mrs. Winterhaven is ready to see you."

"Thank you. Come, Tanya."

I followed her into the office.

"Welcome, Mrs. Delecroie, Miss Delecroie. I have already sent for Hope and Sara. Tanya, I hope that you will join your sisters here one day soon."

"Mrs. Winterhaven, I am sure that Tanya is pleased; however, right now we are just thrilled to have her home. Boarding school is not even on our list for her right now."

There was a knock on the door; then Maggie poked her head in. "The Delecroie girls are here."

"Thank you. Send them in."

I looked at Kerstin nervously and then at the door. It opened and they were standing there, both dressed in the school uniform—knee-length skirts, knee-high socks, and blazers with the school logo. One was in navy blue and the second in hunter green. We looked at each other; then all three of us hugged, and I knew them. I even knew who was who, no questions asked. I just knew.

"When did this happen?"

"Saturday."

"Mom, why did you not tell us?"

"I thought surprising you would be better. Mrs. Winterhaven had to keep you two away from all the news and make sure no one in school said anything."

"Do we have to go back to classes?"

"No, girls, you will go back to the hotel with us, then return tomorrow for your classes."

"Thank you, Mom," they both said in unison. We walked out the door talking about everything and anything.

I looked up at Kerstin on the ride back to the hotel; she was staring at us. I smiled at her, and then quickly rejoined our conversation. Being with Hope and Sara filled a spot in me that I had not known was missing. They say that multiples have a connection that nobody else can even imagine. They are right. Being with my sisters, I was happy. When we got to the hotel, we faced what Kerstin had been trying to avoid. There were reporters lined up in front of the entrance.

"Girls, sit tight. I was afraid of when this would happen. How did they find out so quickly? And that we would have all three together?"

"Mom, it is all right, I will take away all of the attention. You just get the girls inside." Before Kerstin could say anything, Kate had the door opened and it was Kate jumping out. "Ladies and gentlemen, I am surprised that you found out so quickly. However, since you are all here, I will make it official. This afternoon, I did elope with my new husband, William Lord. We thought we would try and hide it by showing up here at different times, but you are onto us."

Kerstin almost choked, but Kate's idea worked, and all the attention went on to her. We all ran into the hotel and up to the room. Kate joined us quickly after; Kerstin was waiting for her.

"Eloped with William? Could you not come up with anything else?"

"Hey, it worked! You should be thanking me."

"Yes, you are right, Honey. Thank you.

"Mom, we are hungry."

"All right, order some room service, something healthy. I need to go call your father."

Kate disappeared into one of the rooms while we sat on the couch talking. Kerstin was just hanging up the phone when the room service arrived. She opened the door and had him set the food on the table. She then looked it over.

"Girls, are you telling me there was nothing healthier on the menu than burgers and fries?"

"Mom, we are celebrating."

"All right, but you will all eat some fruit with it."

"Yes, ma'am."

"Your father and I have decided to go ahead and have a press conference with you three; then hopefully the media will back down."

"When?" Hope asked.

"Tomorrow morning. Your father and Elizabeth are on their way here."

"What do you mean, a press conference?" I asked, confused.

"We go in front of the press; they take our pictures and ask questions."

"Oh."

"Tanya, most of the questions will be asked of you; however, you do not have to answer and you can tell us when you want to go."

"Okay."

We ate our food and then started to get a little rambunctious, running around chasing each other.

"Girls, it is getting late; go get ready for bed."

"But Mom."

"Hope, you have all week, now go."

We all turned and headed to the room we were sharing. Hope and Sara entered, but I turned around.

"Tanya, what is it?"

"Can I call my parents?"

"Yes, but only five minutes; it is getting late, and you have a big day tomorrow."

"Thank you." I went over and picked up the phone. It rang twice before it was answered. "Mommy!"

"Tanya, how are you?"

"I am good. I am with Hope and Sara, and we are having a great time!"

"That is good. Where are you at?"

"In Hartford. We are staying at a hotel."

"It is late there? You should be in bed."

"I am getting ready for bed, but Kerstin let me call you before I went to bed."

"I see she has some sort of sense then."

"Mom, tomorrow we are going to have a press conference. I guess I am famous."

"Yes, your picture has been on TV and in the paper. However, why would they let you have a press conference? They should be shielding you from the media."

"Mommy, they are not going to let anything bad happen to me; besides, the press conference is to get the media to stop following us."

"Well, after what their eldest daughter did, no wonder the media is following them so badly."

"Kate did not elope, she was just distracting the media so I could get inside."

"A life in the spotlight, just what you need."

"Mommy, please do not be mad. I have to go. I love you."

"I love you too, sweetie."

I hung up the phone. I felt guilty now that I was happy with Hope and Sara. I had a connection with them I never expected to have; however, with Mommy and Daddy, they had raised me and were my family that I love.

Kerstin stopped me before I went into the bedroom. "Tanya, what is wrong?"

"Nothing."

"That is not true; you were happy before calling them, and now your smile has disappeared, and your eyes are upset."

"Really, it is nothing."

She took my hand and led me into her room and sat down on the couch.

"We are not leaving this room until you tell me what is wrong."

"I just miss them."

"There is more than that."

"No."

"Tanya, you are my sixth daughter, I have had lots of practice with this, and I know that is goes deeper."

"I just feel guilty for enjoying the time I spent with Hope and Sara."

"So after you spoke with the Johnsons, you were reminded of what you grew up with, and you feel guilty for what you now have."

"Yes...No...I do not know. It is like if I accept them, then I am closing out Sam."

"Just because you enjoy being with Hope and Sara, or even Kate, Ann, and Elizabeth, does not mean you have to close the door on Sam. Sam is the sister that you have spent the last 10 years with; you two have a bond. It is not the same as the bond you have with Hope and Sara, or even the one you will have with your other three sisters. But it is very special, and you should not feel guilty to your sisters here for having a bond with Sam, same as you should not feel guilty to Sam for opening the door for a bond with your sisters here."

"I know but my mo...umm..."

"It is okay for a person to have two moms, and it is okay for that person to love them both. You have known her as your mom for the past ten years also; I would be upset if you did not have a bond with her. The bond you have shows that you were loved deeply, and I am very thankful to her for that."

"She does not think that I should be having a press conference."

"I do not want you to have one either; however, I know that they won't leave you alone until they get what they want, so in your best interest, that is why we have decided to go ahead and do this. I want you to have as close to a normal life as possible. That is why I declined *Dateline*."

"You mean the TV show?"

"Yes."

"They wanted to interview me?"

"Yes, but I declined. Do you feel better?"

"Yes."

"Good, now off to bed," she said, squeezing my hand. I walked back to the room I was sharing with Hope and Sara. They were both asleep, so I changed and climbed into my bed.

I woke up in the morning to a room full of noise. Hope and Sara were just getting up, and through the door, I heard the voices of Craig, Kerstin, and Kate. There were three outfits hanging on the door—one in pink, one in peach, and the third in purple. They each consisted of white blouses trimmed in the respective color, a knee-length skirt, bobbysocks, and matching shoes.

"Do they always pick out the clothes?"

"No, we pick out what we wear at school!"

"But you have uniforms."

"Yes, but we decide what color we wear."

"Wow, you are so lucky!"

"Hey, Sara, looks like Tanya is taking over the role as the funny one."

The door opened and Kerstin appeared. "I thought I heard voices in here. Why don't you get dressed, and I will order your breakfast?"

After we changed, we left the room and sat down at the table. Breakfast consisted of granola and fruit. Kerstin put her hands on my shoulders. "Are you ready?"

"I guess."

"Good. Just remember, let me know when you have had enough, and we will get you out of there."

"All right."

She started braiding my hair. She was finishing up with her third braid when Craig and Kate entered the room. "Good, the girls are ready."

"Hi, Daddy!"

"Hello, Hope, Sara, how is school?"

"Fine, sir."

"How are you, Tanya?"

I just looked at him.

"The press conference is in the ballroom in two hours. I have set up a photo session in the library for the girls."

"A photo session?"

"Yes, so we may release some photos with the conference. Where is Elizabeth?"

"She is still sleeping."

"Kerstin, why did you let her sleep so long?"

"Because she is tired, and this really has nothing to do with her. She is just being dragged along for the ride."

"Will someone get her up?"

"With you yelling like that, you probably just did."

Just then her door opened, and she walked out. "Yes, Father, I am up."

He looked at her then back at Kerstin. "I will take the girls down for the photo session. I will meet you three down there when Elizabeth is ready. Come, Hope, Sara, and Tanya."

The session was kind of fun; there were two photographers taking pictures from different angles. They took pictures of all three of us and then some of them of just me. When they were done, we got to see all of the pictures on the computer. Kerstin chose two to be released; the first one was of all three of us, Hope and Sara sitting on stools, and I was standing behind them. The second was of just me. I was sitting at a desk, my hands folded on a book, and my head turned toward the camera.

Chapter Four

When we entered the room for the press conference, it was filed with reporters and video cameras. On the podium was a line of chairs and two microphones also. Craig went to the microphones; I stood close to Kerstin. Once again all eyes were on me, only this time I was in front of the world. He gave a speech about how they were happy to have me back, and this would conclude my public appearances, that all they wanted for me was to have a normal life. I was too nervous to pay much attention. The next think I realized was that Kerstin and I were next to the microphones, and I was answering the questions.

"How was your childhood? Do you remember being taken? Why did your parents not see all of the publicity? Do you like being a triplet? How has your life changed?"

The one question stuck with me: Why had my parents not seen all of the publicity? I asked Kerstin about that later; she was hesitant but then said that they had probably just had their hands full with two toddlers, and the media was not as large back then.

Hope and Sara did not return to school; instead, we all went to Boston for the day. Craig and Elizabeth returned to California because of Elizabeth's school and exams. We did get up at 6 a.m. on Wednesday. Hope and Sara were going to return to school for their exams. Kerstin wanted to spend the day with me, but I wanted to go to their school and check it out. My outfit was set out for me, surprise! I had a knee-length skirt, a white blouse, and a sweater vest. The plan was that Kerstin would pick us up at 6 p.m. for dinner. Classes at this school were quite different than my pubic school. The classrooms were more like a living room, and no class had more than fifteen girls. The material was more challenging; however, the teachers made it more interesting. The cafeteria was a dining room, and the food was served family style at a long table. Hope and Sara's room was actually an apartment. It had three bedrooms, three baths, and a main living room. Each bedroom was set up with a computer and desk, along with a queen-size bed and matching bedroom set. The main room contained a television, a couch, and two chairs. On the side, were a small table and chairs, along with a mini refrigerator. I participated in the classes and enjoyed myself so much that by the time Kerstin returned, I did not want to go back to the hotel. She agreed to let me stay another day and attend the next day of classes. I was normally bored out of my mind and would do anything to skip.

When I tried to convince Kerstin to let me join the third day, she refused. She wanted another day with just me. Kate had returned to California that morning, so it was just the two of us. She asked me what I thought of the school, but she obviously knew the answer since I was still insisting on going back.

"We have excellent schools in California. Elizabeth's school is similar to this one, and we will have to take you to see it before school starts so you know what to expect."

"Maybe I should go here."

"I think we are going to keep you a little closer to home."

"But Hope and Sara both go here, we get along so great, and I enjoyed the classes."

"Why don't we agree to keep our options open for now?"

I knew that if Hope and Sara were going to go to this school, so was I; they were the two in this family that I connected with. I was thankful when the time came to pick them up from school; I had nothing else to say to Kerstin. We were way past the introduction stage but nowhere near the mother-daughter one. This was their last day of class, so they returned to the hotel with us. This time we each had our own room. We were going to go to New York City on Saturday for some shopping; however, Craig called and told Kerstin she was needed back in California, so we went there instead. The flight was long, and when we arrived, I was tired so I went to my room to relax. I decided I would call Keri and see how she was doing. She was my only remaining factor of my normal life from just one week ago. "Hello, Keri!"

"Well, if it is not Miss Tanya, the most famous girl in the news right now."

"You are kidding, right?"

"Nope, you have been front-page news all week; my favorite was the one "Once and Again, with a Little in Between." It had an infant picture of you, then one of you from home, and then one of you dressed weird sitting at a desk. I have made Grandma take me into town every day so I can get a paper."

"Weird cloths, you mean my new wardrobe?"

"You have to be kidding."

"Nope, and all of my clothes are set out for me."

"We have been picking our own clothes since we were like four."

"I know."

"So do you have your own room, or do you share with your triplet sisters?"

"Well, I do have my own room, but we do share the second-floor west wing."

"What? How big is this place?"

"Buckingham Palace size."

"Wow."

There was a knock at my door, and then a maid appeared.

"Miss Tanya, you have a riding lesson in twenty minutes."

"Keri, hold on. What riding lesson?"

"Your father arranged them for you."

"I do not want lessons."

"You have to take that up with him, Miss."

"Keri, I have to go." I hung up the phone and went to the patio where Kerstin and Craig were sitting.

"I do not want to take riding lessons."

"Tanya, you need to give it a chance."

"Craig, I said I do not want them."

"Well, while you live in this house you will take riding lessons, as well as tennis and piano."

I looked at Kerstin; she was reading a book and ignoring us.

"I would rather be living in a different house, and I am not taking any of those lessons. I would take trumpet; however, you will not let me."

"That is not an instrument for a girl. Now go to the stables for your lesson."

"I am not going."

"Fine. Nancy." He turned to the maid standing in the doorway. "Please have the computer, television, and phone removed from Miss Tanya's room."

"What?"

"If you want the privileges that come with this house, then you will do as I say."

"You should think of me as a person and not a possession," I snapped at him.

"All right, that is enough." Kerstin put her book down and stood up. "Tanya, you will attempt the riding and tennis lessons. If you do not like them, then you may quit. You will take piano lessons; in exchange, you can also take trumpet lessons. Nancy, please leave all of her stuff in her room. Tanya, agreed?"

"I guess."

"Good, now go change and then off to the stables for your lesson."

Riding was actually fun, but I did not want to admit to it since they were making me take the lessons. I went back to my room and fell asleep. I woke up when Hope was knocking on the door.

"Hey, Mom said that she would have our dinner sent up to us. Dad is having a dinner party, and we do not have to attend."

"Good."

"Sara and I are going to eat in her room if you want to join us."

"All right."

Hope walked over to my dresser and was looking at the pictures.

"Is this you and Sam?"

"Yes, that was last Christmas at Grandma and Papa's cabin."

"Was it fun?"

"Yes, Sam and I always had fun together."

"Do you miss her?"

"Yes, and my parents."

"Tanya, this is the last time I am going to say anything about this. If you miss your parents and your sister so much that it hurts, then how do you think everyone here felt? The difference is that you know where they are and can talk to them. Mom and Dad did not know where you were. They could not talk to you or make sure you were happy and warm. That you were alive."

I looked at her; she had a point. But why did Craig think he could run my life? I decided that I would not speak to him again until he treated me as a person and not an object. I ate dinner in Sara's room and then retreated back to my room. I was tired, but I decided that maybe I should call home; I had not talked to them in a while, and Mom had not been too happy the last time I had talked to her.

"Hi, Mom!"

"Oh, so you have not been forbidden to speak to us?"

"No, I was in school."

"What?"

"I went with Hope and Sara to their school."

"Why, are they sending you there?"

"I hope so! Kerstin does not want me to go there, but I really enjoyed it."

"Well, at least she has the sense to say no."

"Well, I want to go, and she will let me."

"Boarding school—that is something we can use when we sue for visitation."

"Mom, I am tired. I am going to go to bed."

We hung up, I changed and crawled into bed.

"Miss Tanya, brunch will be served poolside in 45 minutes."

I got up and changed into the outfit of the day: a white summer dress with purple flowers on it, white sandals, and a purple headband. Sara was walking out of her room at the same time I opened my door; she said that Hope had already gone ahead.

We arrived at the pool house, and everyone was already there, including two people I had not seen yet. One was introduced as William, Kate's soon-to-be husband, and the other as Chris, Ann's boyfriend. Brunch actually ended up being an entire daylong event. I spent most of it swimming and avoiding all conversation with Craig. Soon after I returned to my room, Kerstin appeared. She gave me a schedule that I was to go by during the week. It went as follows:

Monday:	10:00 a.m.	Riding lessons
	3:00 p.m.	Tennis Lessons
Tuesday:	1:00 p.m.	Piano
	3:00 p.m.	Trumpet
Wednesday:	9 a.m.-1 p.m.	Current classes
Thursday:	10:00 a.m.	Riding Lessons
	3 p.m.	Tennis Lessons

Friday:	1 p.m.	Piano
	3 p.m.	Trumpet
Saturday:	10:00 a.m.	Riding lessons

"What are current classes?"

"That is where a tutor comes in, and you have a class so you do not forget what you learn in school."

"I thought summer was for rest and relaxation, but this has me doing stuff every day. What happened to sleeping in or hanging out at the mall? Watching TV all day?"

"The mall does not have enough security, and you need to stay active, let alone keeping up on your studies."

"Well, at least I have my trumpet lessons in there."

"Yes, that reminds me." She went back to the door, picked something up, and came back in. "I thought you might like this."

I opened up the case and inside was a brand-new stradivarius trumpet! "Thank you, this is very cool!"

"Just remember the deal: no piano and then no trumpet."

"I will."

The next morning I started my new schedule; it actually kept me very busy, and when I was not doing a planned activity, I would do something with Hope and Sara, and sometimes Elizabeth.

I dreaded Wednesdays; the tutor was very boring. I was thankful that it was only one day a week. After a month and a half of riding lessons, I was quite good. I talked to Mom and Sam twice a week. They said they were trying to get visitation; however, I never heard anything from Craig or Kerstin about it. Kerstin was impressed at how well I played the piano. I stilled talked to Craig as little as possible; however, with Kerstin I was starting to open up. Wedding plans were being made for Kate and William; it was set for late September. After a lot of arguing, the place was decided on New York City.

Near the end of July, Kerstin came into my room like she did every night; this time was different, though. She sat down next to me and picked up my hand.

"Tanya, I have to go to England for some work. I would like for you, Hope, and Sara to join me."

"England?"

"That will take us up to the point where Hope and Sara return to school."

"You mean all three of us?"

"I do not want you to go so far away to school."

"You would deny me that excellent education for your personal gain?"

"Where did that come from?"

"Watching you."

She smiled at me with a look of being pleased.

"Fine. You may obtain the excellent education for at least one semester. I will be in New York City most of the time this fall, and then we will go from there."

"Thank you!" I called the Johnsons and told them how I was going to England. I avoided calling them Mom and Dad now; my life had changed so much that it felt awkward to call them that. However, I did not call Kerstin or Craig that either; for now, no one filled those shoes. They were not happy that I was going to go so far away; however, they were glad that I was happy.

Chapter Five

We arrived in London a week later. It was much different; well, the manor was similar, but London was different. Everything was prim and proper. I was very excited; however, Hope and Sara could care less. They said that they spend at least a month there every summer and on some of their school breaks. The first few days, Kerstin took me around to see some of the sights. Then I rejoined a schedule of lessons. I did find time to relax and take some long walks through the grounds. One day on a walk, I wondered off the estate, which Kerstin told me not to do. I met a girl named Mary; she lived next door, was also twelve, and an only child.

"My parents cannot wait for me to return to school; my nanny and I are in the way. Do you like your nanny? Mine is okay."

"We do not have a nanny."

"You don't? How many are there?"

"Well, I am a triplet, we are the youngest, and then there is Elizabeth, Kate, and Ann."

"Where do you go to school?"

"I am starting at the Buchanan Academy for Girls."

"I go to Brook Hurst Academy; it is in Scotland. It does not take long to get sent to boarding school, huh?"

"I had to plead to go."

"Why would you want to? Always being told what to do, when to speak and eat. Everything being so impersonal."

"What? The Buchanan Academy is not like that. Classes are interesting, the girls are encouraged to discuss things, and I will have my own room in an apartment I will share with my sisters."

"Your own room? At my school, our rooms are very large; they hold fifty girls per room. Each girl gets a bed and a dresser, and their space is divided by a curtain. Single file lines everywhere you go, no talking in the halls."

"Wow, and your parents send you there?"

"Yes, they do not care. They hardly notice that I am alive."

"That must be rough. I better get back; I am not supposed to be off of the property."

When I returned to the entrance to the grounds, one of the workers was standing there. "Miss, you need to come with me."

I followed him toward the house; when we neared the entrance, the front door opened and Kerstin came running out. "Tanya, thank god. Where have you been?" she said, hugging me.

"I was next door talking with Mary."

She grabbed my wrist and started walking inside. I had never seen her like this. We went into my room. She did not say another word til we got there.

"Tanya, sit down."

I did as she said. I sat down on the edge of the bed and looked at her.

"You had me scared to death. I told you not to leave the property, and then I receive a call saying that you have missed your piano lesson, and you have not been seen in a while. Then I ask your sisters, and they do not have a clue either."

"I am sorry."

"I know you are; however, any of your sisters disobeying me would be facing the consequences. You have been with us now for almost three months, so I am going to have to punish you."

"I am sorry, I will not do it again."

"You are right. Except for your lessons, you are grounded to the house, will be in bed by 9 p.m., and will have no trumpet lessons."

"But all I did was take a walk."

"All you did was take a walk where you were not to go and missed a commitment that you agreed to. I am sorry but that is final."

Although I was upset at first, I realized that she was right; I had not been punished for anything I had done. Kate and Ann had both been threatened to lose their cars and credit cards; Elizabeth, Hope, and Sara had all been grounded. I spent most of the week in my room. Kerstin did take us out for dinner and a show on our last evening in London. They said it was a tradition that they did quite frequently.

The following morning, we left London for Hartford. We arrived mid afternoon. The school was decorated with welcome-back signs, and there was a large dinner planned in the gala room used only for special occasions. We went to the apartment; on the coffee table were a fruit basket and a welcoming card. In my new room, or at least the room I would spend most of the nights in since I had joined this family, hung my uniforms. They came in three colors: maroon, hunter green, and navy blue. There was also one in black.

"Hope, what is this black uniform for?"

"You have a black one?"

"Yes, what is this for?"

"It is for girls selected to be in public democracy…But you have not even gone here yet…It must be a mistake."

"What is public democracy?"

"Public democracy is our student government; they represent the students with the school and do public speaking things. There must be a mistake."

On the desk was a stack of books and also my class schedule:

Tanya Alexandra Delecroie
Age: 12/13 years
Grade: 7th

Classes:	**Mon/Wed/Fri:**	**Tue/ Thu**
8a-9: 30a	American History	English
10a-11: 30a	Algebra	Social Studies
2p-3: 30p	Standard Math	Basic Science
4p-5: 30p	Junior Public Democracy	Junior Public Democracy

"Hope, it says right here: junior public democracy."

"How would you have been selected?"

"I am not sure."

"Mom," she stated, heading toward the door. Kerstin appeared in the hall.

"Tanya has been selected for JPD; how is that possible?"

"Tanya, you were? I am so happy for you! That is quite an honor! Your father will be very pleased."

"But how?" I asked. They both looked at me.

"I do not know; they must have been impressed with your transcripts. Now what other classes do you three have?"

Except for JPD, all of our classes were the same. They had creative arts and governmental theory in its place. We also had a list of the tryout time for all the extracurricular activities. I decided that I was going to go out for soccer, Hope decided on the swim team, and Sara was going to join the theater group. Kerstin joined us for dinner, and then we went back to our room.

"Now girls, I want you to be on your best behavior and enjoy school."

"We will." She gave both Hope and Sara a hug and then sent them off to their rooms. "Now, Tanya, if you do not like it here, call me, and I will be here in a flash."

"I will be fine."

"I know you will be." She opened her purse and pulled out an envelope. "Here, this is for you. Use it if you need anything. I love you very much." She gave me a hug and kissed the top of my head. "I will be back in two weeks."

Then she walked out of the door. I was officially at boarding school! Who would have thought a year ago that I would be in boarding school? I picked up the phone on my desk and called Keri; she was at home by now.

She answered on the second ring. "Are you glad to be back home and off of the farm?"

"YES, but that means I have to go back to school, and it is going to be so different without you there."

"I know; school here is going to be different too. I am going to boarding school in Hartford."

"Ouch. Maybe next summer we can go to boarding school in Switzerland together? I saw Sam today."

"How is she doing?"

"All right; she misses you, I could tell. Your mom had her babysitting for Isabella. The kid is cute."

"I have not seen her; they did send a picture of them all at the beach."

"My parents said that yours are in over their heads with adopting the kid. I guess she has a pretty bad background."

"She is four, how bad can she be?"

"Yes, but your mom is depending on Sam too much."

"Sam will tell her when she has had enough. You know her."

"Yeah."

"I have to get going. I will talk to you later." I hung up the phone and went straight to bed.

I woke up early the next morning, too excited to sleep any longer but also very nervous. I put on the official school uniform in navy, put on a headband, and met Hope and Sara in the living room. We headed down to the dining room at 7 a.m. for breakfast. During my first class, I was very excited to actually be enjoying school. When four o'clock approached, I said goodbye to my sisters and proceeded to the mysterious class of junior public democracy. The instructor's name was Mr. Jacob; this class contained 18 girls, three from each class of seventh and higher.

"Any of our new girls, if you want out of this class, please let me know. This is a six-year commitment, and if you are not willing for that, we will bring in an alternate."

I raised my hand

"Miss Delecroie, you want out?"

"No, I was just wondering why was I chosen for this class? I have not even attended this school."

"Well, Miss Delecroie, first I look at grades; you have a 4.0, and your enthusiasm when you visited us last spring was impressive. At the news conference you had, you presented yourself with confidence. Then your mother told us how you held out until they agreed to send you here. These are all qualities of a leader, and that is why I chose you."

I smiled at him. He then went on to explain the rest of the class. It was divided into two groups—the juniors, grades 7-9, and then the seniors, grades 10-12. The activities we would be doing included presentations and debating. We also would deal with the heads of the school as a voice of the students, and also sit on the panel of disciplinary action against students who broke the rules. As a junior, I would observe in all areas. Then in a few weeks, I would start competing against my fellow classmates on topics and also sit on the panel deciding the punishments of the seventh graders. These were the days that I would wear the black uniform. The meetings were held every other Friday. We stayed in class a little long, and by the time I got back to the apartment, Hope and Sara had already left for dinner, so I met them in the dining room. I told them all about the class. Hope seemed to be a little annoyed at me for talking about it.

The second day in JPD, we were given a topic for a mach debate. Mine was pro for school uniforms. Mr. Jacobs was very impressed when I presented on Friday; I beat my competition (the other seventh graders), so next Friday I was going to compete against the eighth-grade winner.

On Saturday afternoon, they held tryouts for the extracurricular activities. I tried out for soccer. There were four teams: 4th through 6th grades, 7th and 8th grades, 9th and 10th, and 11th and 12th. I made the team as a starting forward. Hope made the swim team, and Sara was very excited about the theater group. They were going to do a show to be performed in early December. I usually had my homework done for my classes during our break in the day, so my evenings were free. The work was challenging but still very easy for me. Hope was starting to get annoyed by that also. I came to the conclusion that she believed since she was the oldest, things should come to her first.

The day of my second presentation—this one about violence on television—I held my ground and won the second debate. Kerstin arrived; she took us all out to dinner. She wanted to know everything we were doing and how we liked it. The next morning, she decided to stop by the office and get both the soccer and swimming schedules. While she was there, she also picked up our progress reports. The teachers turned in new ones every Friday, so they always had an updated progress report in case any parent wanted one at any time. She was impressed that I had straight A's while I was adjusting to the new school, playing soccer, and partaking in Junior Public Democracy. She did have a private talk with Sara. It seems that she had a C in government. They stayed in her room for about a half hour; when they were done, Kerstin stopped by my room and requested that I join her for dinner. It was just the two of us; we went to a small pizza place in town.

"Tanya, are you really enjoying yourself?"

"Yes, I love playing soccer."

"How about your classes? Do you have enough time to complete all of your homework?"

"Yeah, classes are easy; I usually have all the homework done before my next class starts."

"That is good. How are you getting along with your sisters?

"Fine."

"I want you to be warned; this has been their stomping ground for a while, and they are used to having things done a certain way. There may be friction at first, like it is a competition amongst you. Hope's goal was to be in JPD; now you are in it, and she is not too happy about it."

"I did not know that, but there are still five more years; she could be an alternate and get in next year."

"Yes, or the next five years could go by, and she never gets in. You are an optimist, and Hope is a pessimist."

"Oh."

"Anyways, next weekend I will pick you up on Friday morning, and we will go to New York for the weekend."

"But I am debating Andrea; she is in10th grade."

"Oh, well I guess we can wait til after that and just celebrate a little late."

"Celebrate what?"

"Your thirteenth birthday."

"Oh, next Friday is September 5th."

"Yes, it is."

"Hope and Sara probably won't want to wait all day for me."

"Well, it is your birthday also; we will make it up to them, and on Saturday, we can do a shopping spree, a spa treatment, dinner, and a show. Then Sunday, you three will be fitted for dresses to wear at the wedding."

"That sounds like fun."

After dinner, we went back to the school to tell Hope and Sara the plan.

When Kerstin left that night, I gave her a hug. It was not the first time that she had hugged me; however, it was the first time that I had initiated the hug. Until then, whenever she had given me a hug, I had put very little into it.

When she released me, she kissed my forehead and smiled at me. "Tanya, I love you."

I smiled back at her.

The third week of classes went well. I took my first round of test, which was all pretty easy.

When Friday came, I was nervous about the debate, though I forgot all about it at lunch. When we walked into the dining room, there were three cakes on the table. Everyone started singing "Happy Birthday." We celebrated for the next two hours. Then I saw Andrea, and it all came back to me. The presentation. When the time came, Andrea did win. She beat me by four points. However, she also had four years more experience than I did.

I walked back to the dorm to find the unexpected: Craig was there as well as Kerstin. They were sitting on the couch, talking with Hope and Sara.

"Happy Birthday, Tanya."

"Thanks."

"How was the debate?"

"I lost."

Hope got a smile on her face.

"I am sorry, baby."

"It is okay. She does have four years on me, and I picked up some pointers on how to improve for next time."

"Good. Why don't you go put your things away, and we will go to New York."

Less than an hour later, we were in New York City. A limo picked us up and took us to the penthouse in uptown Manhattan. I was impressed by the city. When we arrived at the building, we went to the top floor; it opened up to a massive apartment. Kate, William, Ann, and Elizabeth were all there. Around the room, there were three piles of presents. I was told they had a tradition of opening the presents after they had dinner. I got a tour of the penthouse while we waited for dinner to be finished. The main floor was a living room, family room, dining room, kitchen, maids' quarters, and two bathrooms. Upstairs had five bedrooms and three bathrooms. I was informed that I would be sharing a room with Elizabeth. Hope and Sara shared one; then Kate and Ann each had their own. However, since William was there, Kate would be staying in Ann's room. Dinner was good; then we all went into the living room for presents. Each of the three piles was big enough to be mine and Sam's Christmas presents together. We each received the same general things. The clothes all had the color distinction. I was starting to wonder if Craig would even be able to tell us apart if we did not wear those colors. We also received some books, and I got some soccer things.

The next day we did go to the spa and went shopping. Kerstin bought me a pair of jeans, but she told me that I could never wear them around Craig. For dinner, we went to a very fancy restaurant in mid-town, then off to a show. I was exhausted when we got back to the penthouse.

On Sunday, we went to get fitted for the dresses. It consisted of us standing on a stool and getting measured in every way possible. They said that the dresses would be ready for alterations in eleven days on a Thursday.

"Girls, next Wednesday when you are done with classes, you will come back here. Thursday will be the alterations, Friday the rehearsal, Saturday the preparations, and Sunday will be the wedding at St. Pat's Cathedral with the reception to follow at the hotel."

The dresses were going to be white, mine trimmed in lavender with a lavender shawl; Hope and Sara were going to be the same in pink and peach.

When classes resumed on Monday, I was getting ready for my first soccer game to be held on Saturday against a private school just outside of Hartford. As the week went by, the excitement grew. Saturday morning, I changed into my soccer uniform and headed out to the field. We were going to practice before the game. An hour later, the stands were filling up. I spotted Hope and Sara, and to my surprise, Kerstin was with them. The game went well; I made two goals! And we won.

"Tanya, I had no idea that you were so good!"

"I had no idea that you were coming."

"To admit I almost forgot, but I looked at the schedule yesterday and saw it."

"Thanks."

"Well, why don't you go change, and we will go out and celebrate your win!"

We did, and then Kerstin had to leave. Sunday I relaxed, walked the grounds, and went swimming with Hope and Sara. Monday I decided to get the work I would be missing; I did not want to fall behind. I finished my work, along with going to soccer practice on Monday and Tuesday. I was going to miss my soccer game that weekend, but there was no way I could get a clearance to be there. When we arrived at the penthouse, I ran to my and Elizabeth's room. I found Snowball, a little kitten Elizabeth had found, curled up under a blanket on my bed.

"She has been there all week."

"All week? How do you know that? Are you not going to school?"

"I am, but this term I am going to The Academy here in the city."

"You are? Why?"

"Mom wanted to be here to make sure that the preparations were going well."

"Oh, I see."

"Is there a problem?"

"No, I just do not think that you should have to put up with me crashing in your room every time I come home if you are living here."

"It is our room, and it has been since Dad bought this place. I have always had an extra bed and always been told it is our room; you have every right to be here, and I do not mind."

Everything that weekend was fancy and very formal. Kate and Kerstin were either on the phones or talking with each other. Orders were given, people responding. When Sunday morning finally arrived, the penthouse did not know the meaning of silence. I stayed in Hope and Sara's room. Kerstin knocked on the door when it was time to go to the church. She was upset that our hair had not been done; then she realized that she was the one to do it. When we got to the church, she recruited Ann to help her. As they French braided our hair, they added small flowers to it that matched the color of our dresses. St. Pat's was huge and it was packed full. There were even televisions so the people in the back could see what was going on a little better. Then we went to the hotel for the reception. William's family was all fascinated by how many sisters Kate had, but I think it was more with the "triplets" than anything. Craig gave them the honeymoon suit at the hotel for the night and then a three-week trip to Austria.

It was after 11 p.m. when we left the reception; I was so tired that I fell asleep in the limo. Kerstin was carrying me when I woke up.

"Where are we?"

"Almost home." She put me down in the elevator and put her arm around me. "Let's get you to bed." I was sound asleep when Elizabeth came in.

We were allowed to sleep in the next morning. By the time we got to school, it was after 3 p.m. We did not have to go to our classes, but I decided to still go to JPD. Everyone welcomed me back and asked lots of questions about the wedding. I had a soccer game on Wednesday and Saturday, practice the rest of the nights. I also had a research project, a paper, and a piano recital. I found this was, so far, my busiest week. As the projects became more, I was feeling more and more tired. I started replacing the formal meals with a quick snack when I remembered. We won our soccer games, I got an A on the paper and the project, and the recital went well also. The following week was pretty much the same: two soccer games, two exams, a research project, and a paper. By Thursday afternoon, I was exhausted. I fell asleep at my computer. When I woke up, it was 1 a.m., and I still had to type the paper. Before I knew it, Hope and Sara were going to breakfast.

"Tanya, are you coming?"

"No, I have just a little left."

"You skipped dinner yesterday."

"I will get a bite to eat before class."

I finished right before class started, so I did not have time to get anything. We handed in our papers, and then class was dismissed. I picked up my bag and went to stand up.

Chapter Six

When I woke up my head hurt. I was in a bit of a haze. I opened my eyes and saw Kerstin. I was lying in a bed, and I had an IV in my arm. "Where am I?"

"You are in a hospital; you are in New York."

"What happened?"

"You were sick; you pushed yourself too far. You fell and hit your head on the corner of a desk, then on the floor. You have a concussion and have been in a coma."

"What? How long?"

"Let's let the doctor check you out."

"How long?"

"Three weeks."

"What! Three weeks, what about?"

"Tanya, calm down," said a man walking in the door. "How do you feel?"

"My head hurts. How far behind am I?" I looked at Kerstin.

"Do not worry about anything. I am going to give you a quick exam. Do you want your mom here or gone?"

"I want her here."

"All right." He gave me a full checkup. Kerstin held my hand the whole time. "Mrs. Delecroie, she seems to be doing much better; we will keep her a few more days, then I do not see any reason why we will not be able to release her as long as you follow what we spoke about."

"Keep me here? Why?"

"Just to make sure you are okay."

"I am fine. I have so much work to catch up on." I tried to sit up.

"Tanya, do not worry about it."

"But." I grabbed at the IV in my arm.

"Mrs. Delecroie, I am going to sedate her."

I lay back down.

"No, please, I will calm down."

The doctor had the needle next to me.

"Mom, please."

He looked from me to her, then I looked at her.

"What? Why are you staring at me?"

"Tanya, you called me Mom."

"I did?"

"Yes. Doctor, please wait; if she calms down, I see no need to sedate her."

He smiled at her and left the room.

"You said we are in New York?"

"Yes, they have a much better facility here to handle a head trauma. Your sisters and father have all been coming by to see you. Now close your eyes and rest."

I did as she said; I fell right asleep. When I woke up again, it was dark; Kerstin was still there, however, and so was Kate.

"I am hungry."

"All right, baby, I will have someone bring you up something."

The food they brought tasted worse than it looked and did not look very good in the first place. "Hope and Sara will be here to see you tomorrow."

"What day is it?"

"Friday, October 29th."

"Oh." I lay back against the pillow. "I am going to close my eyes; my head hurts."

"Okay, baby, we are going to go so you can get some sleep."

"NO, please don't leave me." The one stable thing in my life right now was that she loved me, would protect me, and I felt safe with her around.

She brushed her hand over my cheek. "All right, baby, I will just walk

Kate to the elevator; then I will be right back." I was asleep by the time she came back.

They kept me in the hospital until Monday. Over the weekend, everyone came to visit me. I was surprised that Craig did not try and give me some sort of lecture about all of this. On Monday, when they took me back to the Penthouse, all of my stuff had been moved into Kate's room.

"This is your new room; I want you to lie down for a while."

"What about Kate?"

"We gave her and William and apartment downstairs, and we decided to move you into her old room. Now lie down. I will be back in a while to check on you."

I was home for the next week. I had a lot of free time on my hands; I used the time to catch up on my homework. In the evenings, Elizabeth and Kerstin and I would play board games. She finally agreed to let me return to school a week later. I think it had more to do with my constant nagging about when I could go back that made her give in. It was agreed that I could not miss a single meal, I had to see the school nurse every day, take the medication provided, and I had to contact her if I felt ill in any way. She seemed very nervous about letting me return to school. I knew the only reason she finally said yes was because it was what I wanted. If I did not follow her guidelines and conditions, she said she would pull me from school.

Being back to school kept me very busy. I fell back into my old routine easily. I was careful not to miss a meal; I did not want to be pulled from school. Hope and Sara were watching me carefully and always asking if I was okay. A week after I was back, I had had enough. I was sitting in the living room by the coffee table working on my homework when Hope came in. I looked up at her and smiled. "Hi."

"Hi, Tanya. How are you?"

"Fine."

"Have you had a snack?"

"Hope, please."

"Well, the nurse just stopped me and said that you did not come in."

"Are you my keeper?"

"Mom just asked me to..."

"Stop it, just stop it. I am fine, my head does not hurt, and I do not need the aspirin."

"Mom just wants me to keep an eye on you."

At that moment, the phone rang. It was sitting next to me so I answered it.

"Hello?"

"Hi, baby. How do you feel?"

"Fine."

"The nurse called and said that you have not been in to see her yet today."

"Why is my life a public record? I feel fine. With everyone freaking out around me, I think I am the only one who does not need a doctor."

"Calm down, I told the nurse to call me if you had not seen her by 5 p.m. So you feel okay without having taken you medication?"

"Yes."

"Good, I am glad; however, you still have a weakened immune system. I do not want anything to happen to you; please go see the nurse and take your medication."

"Why do I have to see the nurse every day? Why can't I just have it here?"

"It is only for another two weeks."

"Can you at least tell Hope and Sara to back off?"

"I can do that, but they will still tell me if you skip a meal."

"Okay."

"Baby?"

"Yeah?"

"How was your day? School okay?"

"Yes, it is fine, not really much of anything happening."

"So have you been having fun?"

"As much as anyone will let me."

"Give yourself some time. How are your sisters?"

"Fine. Sara went to the stables, and Hope is sitting here eavesdropping."

"I am not."

"See, I told you."

"Well, why don't you let me talk to Hope. I will talk to you soon?"

"Okay."

"Tanya, I love you. Don't forget our deal."

"I won't." I handed the phone across to Hope who was now sitting across from me doing her homework.

"Hi, Mom," she said, taking the phone from me. I went back to my homework while they talked. When they hung up, our previous topic was dropped.

A half hour later, Sara came in. "Hi, guys! I am starved; are you two ready for dinner?"

"Sure, I am. Tanya?"

"You two go. I have to go see the nurse first."

"We will walk with you."

When we went to see the nurse, she went overboard. Instead of just giving me my medications, she wanted to take my temperature, my blood pressure, and the works. It was another half hour before we finally got to dinner.

The rest of the week went along smoothly. Before I knew it, I only had three days left before we were out on our Thanksgiving break. Most of the girls were going to stay at the school for the holiday; we were only getting out for two days, then the weekend. We were busy doing our final projects because when school resumed, we would be taking our exams. Then off for Winter Break! On Wednesday when my final class was over, I walked back up to the apartment. When I opened the door, Craig was sitting on the couch.

I looked around. "Where is Mom?" I felt weird calling her "Mom," but after the hospital, I felt weird calling her Kerstin now also.

"Nice to see you, Tanya. Is that any way to greet your father?"

"Sorry, hi. Where is Mom?"

"How about, 'hello, Father,' and then a hug?"

I put my bag down and realized that it was going to be a long day.

"Hello, Father," I said and gave him a hug. "Where is Mom?"

"Your mother is in a meeting with the headmistress; she will be back shortly."

The door opened and Hope and Sara appeared. They both looked at each other and then at him, both greeting him the way I just done.

"Girls, your mother will be back in a little while; why don't you get what books and thing you will need ready to go."

I went to my room and sat down at my desk, putting some things in my bag. When I was done, I looked up. Mom was standing in the doorway, leaning against the side. I smiled at her.

"I could watch you all day." She came over and gave me a hug, then took my hand and led me toward the bed and sat down. "You are doing okay?"

"Yes."

"Good."

"What is wrong?"

"Nothing for you to worry about."

"Then tell me, why were you meeting with the headmistress?"

"Honey, do not worry about it. Now, what do you want to take with you?"

"Not much, I will be back on Sunday."

"Baby, you are not coming back."

"What are you talking about?"

"I have decided to keep you at home."

"I have kept up my end of the deal; I am doing everything you asked. Why would you break your end of the deal?"

"Things are going to be very hectic; you need to relax. And take it easy."

"I am not leaving if I am not coming back."

"Sweetie, please do not do this. Why don't we discuss it when we get back to New York?"

"No. You are being carried away with this. I hit my head, and I have been fine for a month now; why is everyone still walking on eggshells around me?" I said, standing up.

"We are not."

"Yes, you are, and you would not deny it unless…" I paused, then turned back to look at her. "Unless there is something wrong."

"Baby."

"What is it?"

"Do not worry about it."

"Tell me NOW!" I said and sat back down in my chair at my desk.

"All right, but you have to calm down and stay calm."

"Now you are scaring me."

"You are sick. It was more than just a fall from hunger and exhaustion. You have leukemia."

"That is cancer."

"Yes, the pills you have been taking are a new treatment. Your doctor thought we could give it a try before we put you through anything else."

"Does everyone know except me?"

"No, Hope and Sara do not know. The rest of your sisters do know, however."

"Why did you not tell me?"

"I did not want you to worry."

"How long were you going to keep this from me?"

"I do not know. I just want you to be normal after everything you have already been through." She walked over and put her arms around me.

"Why am I not being allowed to come back after the holiday?"

"You need rest and relaxation, not the stress of this place."

"I can relax and still take my exams. I would be less stressed here, knowing that I am not falling behind in school than I would be in an apartment with lots of free time to worry about everything."

She started stroking my hair. "Sweetie, we will talk about it at home."

"I do not want them to know."

"We will keep it between us; I will not tell your other sisters that I told you."

"Okay."

"Now," she said, opening her purse, "I have your pills, and I believe it is time for you to take them." She handed me two pills and a small bottle of water. I looked at them for a moment and then put them in my mouth. "That is my girl. Are you ready to go back to New York?"

When we arrived at the penthouse, Elizabeth and Ann were in the den; Kate met us at the elevator. When we walked through the door, Ann and Elizabeth came out to greet us; then Mom sent us to bed.

"But it is only 8:30 p.m."

"Hope, I know; however, you have a big day tomorrow, so off to bed."

I decided not to join in on the complaining game, so I said goodnight and went to my room. I changed then crawled into bed. Snowball, the little kitten, followed me and curled up on the end of my bed. I started reading my book.

At 9 p.m., Mom knocked on my door. "Baby, do you have any other questions?"

"What if this does not work?"

"Then we will have to change your treatment."

"When will that happen?"

"You have a checkup on Friday, which should give us some idea."

"Friday?"

"Yes, Friday morning. Now why don't you lie down and rest?"

I closed my book and lay back.

"I love you; everything is going to be okay." She kissed my forehead and then left the room, shutting off the lights as she shut the door.

I lay there in the dark. One more thing to add to my already hectic life. Why me? Why was I the sick one? Why was I the one to be kidnapped? Why was I the one to be found? Why me? Would I get better? What if I did not?

I felt a hand on my head, so I opened my eyes.

"Good morning, baby!"

"What are you doing?"

"You are warm."

"I am fine."

"Well, I was getting worried that you were not up yet, so I came to check on you."

"Up yet? What time is it?"

"Ten-thirty."

"So I was tired." I sat up, forcing her to remove her hand.

"Maybe I should take you to the hospital."

"I am fine."

"I am going to take your temp."

"Mom."

'That or straight to the hospital."

"Fine." She left the room and returned with a thermometer. I was at the closet when she walked in and stuck it in my ear for an instant reading.

"99.9, you do have a temp."

"I feel fine; it is not that big of a temp."

"I do not care, back into bed."

"But…"

"Tanya Alexandra. NOW!" I did as she said, not wanting to argue. "I am going to get you some orange juice and toast. I will be back in a moment." She walked out and shut the door. I turned on the TV and watched the parade. She did return shortly with the toast and orange juice.

"I am fine, really."

"We will let the doctor decide on that."

"Can't I go watch TV with Hope and Sara?"

"No, I do not want you around anyone; you could get their germs."

"Will you stop being paranoid?"

"I am trying to protect you. Please eat your toast." I stared at her, and then I finally picked up a piece and took a bite. "Thank you. Now rest."

"Are you going to let me come out and eat dinner with the family?"

"No, I do not want you around others."

"So, you are going to make me spend my first Thanksgiving with this family locked away in my room instead of with my family, whom I have not been with in over 10 years?" That seemed to do the trick.

"If you get worse, you will be in here all weekend."

"Fine."

She took my hand and looked at me. "Let's go." We went into the den. "Look who is feeling better."

"Hey, Tanya."

I felt her hand rubbing my back; then she whispered in my ear, "Please take it easy."

"I will."

She kissed the top of my head and left the room. I sat down next to Hope.

"What was wrong? She came in here a little while ago said that you were sick and she did not want us to go to your room."

"I woke up with a fever, and she went overboard." I picked up a pillow and hit her with it; I wanted to change the subject. It worked; before long, we were having a pillow fight and laughing.

Thanksgiving dinner was a full seven-course meal. I was actually becoming so used to this lifestyle that it did not even surprise me. By the time the meal was over, I was tired. Ann was going down to Kate's for some evening entertainment; Hope, Sara, and Elizabeth all wanted to watch a movie.

"I am going to go to bed; I am kind of tired."

From nowhere, Mom appeared with her hand going straight to my forehead. "You are warm again; I should not have let you come out for dinner."

"I am fine; Turkey makes you tired from that chemical they put in it, that is all."

She gave me a long look. "All right, off to bed then. Do not forget you have an appointment tomorrow."

"I know."

The next morning, we arrived at the doctor's office at 11 a.m. sharp. He ran several tests on me.

"Tanya, have you been tired? Loss of appetite?"

"No."

"Yesterday, she woke up with a fever and was in bed by 8 p.m."

"Tanya, if we are going to help you, we need to know the truth."

"I have been busy, nothing out of the normal."

"All right." He ran a few more tests and then went to get the results from the first set.

"Mrs. Delecroie, why don't you and I step into my office?" She nodded at him.

"NO, I want to know."

She looked at me, then took my hand. "She should know."

Now he nodded his head. "Tanya's leukemia has not advanced; however, the medication has not had the progress that I was hoping for." He paused; Mom slipped her arm around me. "I want to increase her dosage; hopefully that will give us better results."

"What if is does not?"

"Tanya, you do not need to worry about that."

"I would like to know."

He looked at mom and then back to me. "If this does not work, we will have to put you in the hospital, put you on several very strong medications that will weaken your immune system, and then give you a bone marrow transplant from one of your sisters."

"Oh."

"But that is way off."

"On this new medicine, am I going to be all right at school?" Mom looked at me; she knew what I was doing.

"Yes, you should have no problems as long as you take it easy. A slight fever will be normal, and you will find that you are going to tire easily." Then he looked at Mom. "If her temp goes over 100, then make sure she goes to bed, and call me if it goes higher."

"Thank you, doctor." She took me out to lunch before we went home. Saturday Hope and I went to see a show while Sara stayed at home to finish her homework. Sunday morning we had brunch in the dining room; the subject of school came up.

"What time are we leaving to go back today?" I asked.

Mom and Craig both looked at each other. After a few moments of silence, she opened her mouth. "At four." It was official! They were letting my go back! I smiled at them.

When she dropped us off at school, I went to my room and put my things away. She followed me and shut the door. "I am not thrilled about you being here."

"Really? I could not tell."

"We still do not know how you are going to react to this new medication."

"I will be fine."

"Still, I have ground rules for you. You eat every meal. If you feel sick, call me. If you get a temp, call me. Only class and be in bed by 9 p.m."

"Mom."

"Tanya, there is nothing that I would like more than to take you home with me right now, but I know that you want to be here, so these are the terms. Do we agree?"

"If I do call you for a small thing, are you going to pull me out of here?"

"I will only pull you if your doctor advises to, or I find out you did not call me."

"Fine, deal."

She put her arms around me and pulled me into a hug, "I love you, baby."

"I love you too." She held me tighter. This was the first time I had said that to her.

"I will see you in two weeks." She kissed my forehead and walked out.

Chapter Seven

The next two weeks went quickly. I called three times to say I had a slight fever, but I was fine. There was a big snowstorm, so we had to start taking the underground tunnels to get to the main building. All of the dining and common rooms had fires going in the fireplaces, and they also started serving us hot chocolate and hot cider. The days dwindled by until we were down to our last day of classes and last set of exams. Mom was picking us up after classes and then taking us home. Which home, I was not sure. My last exam was not as difficult as I had thought it was going to be. When I was through, I met up with Hope and Sara in our apartment; they were talking about Christmas. We told each other stories about our previous Christmas. When Mom arrived, she told us that we would be spending the holiday in California. When we arrived, I was very tired. Hope and Sara were both already asleep; they were carried inside while Mom walked with me up to my room. I climbed into bed and fell fast asleep.

When I woke up, I walked around the room. I had forgotten how big it was. The room in New York was big, but this was huge! I got dressed and walked down to the den. Kate and Mom were in there.

"Good morning, Tanya."

"Hi."

"I thought that I would take all of my girls shopping today. How does that sound, Tanya?"

"Like fun!"

"Good. Now sit down and have breakfast with us."

I sat down; she handed me some pills. I took them and drank some water. The whole time Kate was watching me; I looked at Mom, then at her. "Kate, I know."

"You do?" she said, then looked at mom for confirmation, who nodded. "What about…?"

"No, I do not want them to worry."

"Okay."

After a while, everyone had joined us. We left at 10 a.m. Mom gave each of us some spending money. I counted ten $100 bills in my hand. My jaw dropped; I had never seen that much money at one time. We split up; Elizabeth went by herself, Hope went with Kate, Ann and Sara were together, and I went with Mom.

"Now remember, we will meet back here in three hours. Keep your phones on and have fun!"

I was starving by the time the we met back up. Mom decided that we were going out to lunch; she took us to a little ritzy place. The food was good; however, I thought the people were a bit snobby. When we arrived back at the manor, I was amazed to see the Christmas tree. It had been put up while we were out. It stood 15-feet high. I went up to my room and wrapped all of the gifts that I had purchased. Then I lay down on the couch.

"Tanya."

I opened my eyes. The room was dark, and Mom was kneeling next to me.

"Yes?"

"Do you feel all right?"

"Just tired."

"You have been asleep for at least four hours."

"I have?"

"Yes, do you think you can eat something?"

"Yeah."

She walked over to the phone and ordered a dinner tray. I sat up on the couch. I decided that I would buy my other parents some gifts on the Internet and have them shipped to them. I also decided that I was not going to tell them that I was sick. No sense in having them worry about it when they could not do anything. After I ate my dinner, I changed into my pajamas and went back to bed. The next morning, I felt 100% refreshed. Hope and I played board games, and I went swimming with Sara.

The days til Christmas were getting shorter; I was getting very excited like I had when I was little. Two days before Christmas, Mom came into my room at night just as I was getting ready for bed.

"Hi, Mom, what is going on?"

"I just wanted to talk to you."

"About what?"

"I was just thinking about the last seven months. You have changed so much. I was so afraid when I brought you here; you did not smile or laugh. Then you opened up, and I loved seeing the joy in your face. When we found out that you were sick, I was afraid all over again. I could not stand to lose you again. These last few days I have been watching you. Your face is a permanent smile, and your laugh is contagious."

"I guess I have changed."

"You guess. Tanya, please tell me the truth. Are you happy?"

"Am I happy?" I paused for a moment. I guessed I was. "Yes. When I first came back, all I wanted was to go home; I wanted to be with my sister and my parents. I still miss my other family. But yes, I am happy."

"Good, I am glad. Watching you these last few days has made me more excited for Christmas than I have been in eleven years." I smiled at her. "Now tomorrow, you, your sisters, and I are going to the children's hospital to give away presents."

"Okay."

She kissed the top of my head. "I love you, baby."

"You too."

Nancy woke me in the morning; she had my breakfast on the table. I changed, then sat down to eat. Mom came in when I was finishing up. "Good morning, how did you sleep?"

"Good."

She handed me two pills; I took them without saying anything.

When we arrived at the children's hospital, I was surprised to see how large it was. The windows and halls were filled with pictures of Santa and the North Pole. We were walking down the hall when I saw a girl my age sitting in a room all alone. I walked in to talk to her.

"Hi, I am Tanya."

"I'm Jenny."

"What do you want for Christmas?"

"My mom back."

"Oh, What happened to her?"

"She died in the accident."

"I am sorry."

"Sure you are. After today you are going to go back to your huge home you have grown up in and pat yourself on the back because you did your charity work for the year, then continue to live your spoiled life. I will end up in a foster home when I get out of here, so excuse me if I do not embrace your perfect life."

"I do not have a perfect life. I grew up in a small, two-bedroom house, then I found out I had been kidnapped. I was taken and sent back to live with a family I did not even know. After I was settling in, we found out that I have leukemia. I have no idea what is going to happen. I could be in that bed next week for all I know."

She looked at me in amazement. "Actually, cancer patients are one the third floor." She smiled at me, then we both started laughing. By the time we left, I had decided that there was no use in feeling sorry for myself. There were so many people worse off than I was.

After dinner, Hope, Sara, and I were all very excited! Too excited to sit still. So we were running from room to room, laughing and yelling.

"All right, girls, come in here!" Mom yelled as we ran past the living room.

"Yes, Mom?" we all replied in unison, still laughing.

"I am glad that you are having fun; however, I think you all need to head off to bed."

"But Mom, it is only 8 p.m."

"Hope, I know what time it is, but after you get ready for bed, it will be later."

"Mom, like twenty minutes? We are having fun," Sara replied. I sat down on the piano bench. There was a pause. I looked up and saw she was looking at me.

"All right, you may stay up if you all agree to stay in here and for Tanya to play some Christmas music."

"I do not want to."

"All right, off to bed."

Hope and Sara both looked at me. I knew they wanted to stay up, so I turned around and started playing. Craig, Kate, William, Ann, and Elizabeth all joined us. After forty-five minutes, I was tired of playing, and just plain tired. I excused myself and was asleep before my head hit the pillow.

"Wake up! Come on, wake UP! It is Christmas morning!"

"Okay, I am, quit jumping on me," I said, hitting her with my pillow.

"Sara went to go wake up Mom and Dad," she said as she threw my robe and slippers at me.

"Okay, I will meet you downstairs. I want to make a phone call." She nodded and left.

I picked up the phone and dialed my other home. There was no answer, which was weird, so I left a message then ran downstairs. I was astonished when I entered the room; under the tree had to be three hundred presents. The stockings were overfilled with gifts.

I heard Mom laughing. "Merry Christmas, Tanya!" I looked at her; she came over and gave me a hug.

"Wow, I have never seen so much," I said as we walked to the couch.

"Yes, you have, you just do not remember." Within a few moments, everyone was there and we started opening presents. It took an hour and a half to open all of the gifts. I received a new game boy with fifteen games, a DVD player, several books, new clothes, some soccer things, and also some jewelry. Mom was in charge of the meals since they had given the entire staff the day off. After we ate, Mom sent us up to change. I chose to wear one of my new jumpers. I met Hope and Sara in the hall. We all started laughing. The one time we were all allowed to pick out our own clothes, we all chose the same thing.

"Great minds think alike!"

We returned to the living room and played with our new things. Mom sat and watched us. I knew her eyes were on me, but I did not care. I looked up at her and smiled. I finally realized what they had been trying to tell me. I had not wondered what they were doing because I had not remembered them, but they would have sat here watching Hope and Sara, wondering what I was doing. Was I happy? And loved? I could not understand before, but now I could. I had grown to love them, and now I could not see my life without them. I walked over and sat down next to Mom.

"What is wrong, baby?"

"Nothing, everything is just fine."

She put her arm around me, I lay my head on her shoulder, and that was one Christmas I knew I would not forget.

The day after Christmas, things were getting back to normal. All of the employees were back, and Mom was hovering over me. "Tanya, we are leaving for New York tomorrow."

"We are spending New Years there?"

"No, we will be back in a few days. You have a doctors appointment."

"So it is just you and I going?"

"Yes."

"What are you going to tell Hope and Sara?"

"You and I are spending some one-on-one time."

The flight was long, but I watched a movie to occupy some of the time. The penthouse was empty with just the two of us; it was late when we arrived, so I went to bed.

She took me to breakfast before my appointment. The doctor ran the same test as before. Then he returned with the results.

"Mrs. Delecroie, Tanya, I do not have very good news." Mom squeezed my hand. "We cannot increase the dosage any more. Her body is becoming immune, and the leukemia is starting to advance."

"So where do we go from here?"

"We need to put her on radiation and chemo, and prepare her for a bone marrow transplant." Mom wrapped her arms around me.

"What do you mean by transplant?"

The doctor looked at me. "Tanya, you are lucky; you have two identical sisters. The three of you all have the same genetic makeup, so we can use one of them."

"But what are you going to do?"

"First, we put you in the hospital, we put you on chemo and radiation, and then after a while, we bring in one of your sisters. Your immune system will be very weak from the rest of the medication that we have to give you to prepare you. Then when your ready, we will bring in one of your sisters, take the marrow from her, and then transplant it into you. Then hopefully the new bone marrow will help your body produce its own healthy marrow."

"How long?"

"You will be in the hospital for about three weeks, maybe longer."

"Then I will be better?"

"No, but it will be a start. We are hoping that this will put you into remission. After five years in remission, then you will be deemed cured."

"Oh."

He looked back at Mom. "We should get her started as soon as possible, Mrs. Delecroie."

She started playing with my hair. “Tanya and I are going back to L.A. tomorrow. We will stay there and spend the holiday with the family, and then I will bring the girls back here. We can start her on the 2nd.”

“All right, I will have everything scheduled for five days from now.”

“Doctor, I want to make sure that she has the best of everything.”

“I will take care of it.”

“Thank you.” She took my hand and we went to the limo.

“Why don’t we go shopping, to dinner, and then to a show?”

“Okay.” I was not in the mood for it; however, I knew it would not be happening again soon. When the limo pulled away, she took out her cell phone and called Craig. Listening to the one side of the conversation, it sounded as if he was going to tell Hope and Sara. When she hung up, I wanted to know.

“Is he telling Hope and Sara?”

“Yes, we think they need to know now, especially Hope. We have decided that we will use her since she is the oldest.”

“Oh.” I turned my head and watched out of the window.

When we were shopping, Mom bought me anything that I expressed any interest in. At dinner she let me have dessert—ice cream and a brownie—when normally we are not allowed to have many sweets. Then she bought tickets to see my favorite show. I fell asleep in the limo on the ride back.

I woke up in my bed. My room was dark; I looked around and noticed that Mom was asleep in the chair. The last time I had found her asleep next to me had been when I was in the hospital. I rolled over and went back to sleep. When I woke up in the morning, she was gone.

Mom tried to occupy me on the flight back, but I had too much on my mind. Hope and Sara were waiting for us when we arrived.

“Why did you not tell us?”

“I don’t know.”

“Well, now you are stuck with us.”

I looked at them, then around. “Let’s go swimming.”

Everyone looked at me with a little surprise. But that is what we did. Craig even ordered pizza for us! The next two days we played games, watched movies, and spent a lot of time in the pool. On New Years, Craig threw a party. We all tried to avoid it, but Mom caught us and made us come back into the ballroom. We sat in the corner for the remaining part of the evening, making polite conversation. By the time midnight came around, I was exhausted. Mom came over and sent us all to bed anyways.

The next morning, we left for New York; everyone came. At the penthouse, I went to my room and shut the door. Everyone had been crowding around me all day. I needed some time to myself. I also decided to give my other family a call before I went into the hospital; I did not know when I would be able to do so again.

"Hi!"

"Hi, Tanya. How are you?"

"Fine. I just wanted to say Happy New Years!"

"You too."

"How is everyone?"

"Good. Sam and your dad are in Mexico—an unexpected business trip."

"Oh."

"How was your Christmas?"

"Good, I got some books, games, and some clothes."

"That is nice. Where did you spend the holiday?"

"In California."

"So you are here now?"

"No, I am now in New York."

"Oh, they could not stay in one place."

"No, I have something I wanted to do here."

"You do? What?"

"Nothing important. I need to get ready for bed; I will talk to you soon."

"I love you."

"Love you too." I hung up the phone and paused by it.

"Did you tell her?"

"No." I turned around. Kerstin was standing in the door. "How long have you been there?"

"Not long, I just wanted to see how you were doing."

"I am fine."

"Is there anything you want to take to the hospital with you?"

"I am not sure."

"I have gotten you some new pajamas and some books."

"Thank you. May I take some pictures?"

"Yes, of course."

I walked over to my dresser. I picked up two of them, and one of Hope, Sara, and me in front of school; the other was of Mom and me in London. I handed them to her.

She looked down at them then smiled. "Everything is going to be fine."

"I know."

"Are you ready for tomorrow?"

"As much as I can be. When is Hope going to go in?"

"She will be admitted after your marrow is almost gone."

"Will we be able to be in the same room?"

"No, baby. You are going to be in isolation."

"So nobody will be with me?"

"I will be with you; I'll be in gowns from head to toe. But I will be with you."

"Good."

"It is okay to be scared."

"I know."

Then she gave me a hug. "All right, you need to get into bed."

"Okay." I climbed into my bed; she pulled the covers over me and kissed my forehead.

"I love you, baby."

Then I was alone.

Chapter Eight

Mom woke me up 6 a.m. She handed me a pair of jeans and a sweatshirt, then smiled at me. I changed. I was hungry, but the doctor had told her not to let me eat before coming into the hospital. We arrived at the hospital a little after 7 a.m.; Craig held a press conference announcing that he was making a donation to the hospital while Mom took me in the other side of the hospital. That way I could get in without a lot of people having knowledge that I was there. They took me to a room; it had one bed in the center of it. It was a typical hospital room. I got into the bed, and they hooked three IV's to my arm. The drugs made me tired and nauseous. Mom was by my side just like she promised.

"How is she doing?"

"She's doing okay; she is strong."

"The girls all send their love to both of you."

"Thank you, I will tell her when she wakes up."

"Good. Have you gotten any sleep?"

"Yes, she is out most of the time. The rest she is throwing up. How is Hope doing?"

"Good, I am bringing her in tomorrow. She is a bit nervous."

"She will only be here one night?"

"Yes, I told Sara that she could stay with Hope; Sara is feeling a bit down."

"That will be good for both of them."

My eyes were heavy. I knew that I should open them, but then they would quit talking. I wanted to know what was going on. If they were brining in Hope already, then I had been there for how long? A week? Just then my stomach turned; I was going to be sick.

"Mom."

Instantly she was standing next to me with a bowl. She rubbed my back. "It is okay, you are going to be just fine." When I had lain back down, she took the bowl away and returned with a glass of water. "Here, drink this."

I shook my head no; I did not want to eat or drink anything.

"Yes, Tanya, you need to stay hydrated. Sit up and drink this."

I sat back up; she helped me with the glass. Craig was standing next to the window, watching the whole thing. After I drank some water, I lay back down and closed my eyes. Mom brushed my hair aside, then put a cold washcloth on my forehead.

"Is that normal?"

"Yes. It really started getting bad about two days ago; then she just falls back asleep."

"Hopefully this will work, and then we can put this into the past."

"I just want to know why it is always her? I mean, I do not want any of my children to suffer, but why her? She was the one who was not breathing when they were born, the one kidnapped, and now the one with leukemia?"

"I do not know, Kerstin."

When I woke up again, Craig was gone and so was Mom. I felt sick and started crying. The door opened and Mom came running in.

"I am sorry, baby. I stepped out to speak with the nurse." She rubbed my back until it was over, then got me a glass of water to drink. This time when I lay back down, she laid next to me and wrapped me in her arms.

"Good morning, Tanya," a nurse dressed head to toe in gowns said.

"Where is my mom?"

"She is changing into her gowns; your immune system is getting too weak to fend off anything, so we sterilized the room."

"Oh."

"Are you up for some breakfast?"

"No."

"Well, we will see. Your sister is being admitted today."

"I know."

"Do you like always having someone to play with?"

"Yes."

Mom reentered the room; she was dressed like the nurse. Only her eyes were showing.

"Mrs. Delecroie, could you please talk to your daughter, maybe get her to eat something?"

Mom looked at me, then replied, "Not a problem." The nurse left, and Mom wheeled the tray over to the bed, then put my bed into a sitting-up position. "Now, you need to eat."

"What is the point? It will just come back up in an hour."

"You need to keep up your strength, and that means eating." She picked up the spoon and filled it with pudding. "I can feed you like I did when you were a baby."

I started laughing, then took the spoon from her.

"That is my girl. It is good to see you laugh."

I finished the pudding and went back to sleep.

"Mom." The routine started over again. She took my hand when I lay back down. "It is almost over, baby, and soon you will feel better."

"They have just finished with Hope; she is in recovery, and she is asleep."

"Let me know when she is back in her room so I can go see her."

"All right, I better get back down there. Kate is sitting with her right now."

"Good, I do not want either of them to be alone."

I was watching them, but they did not realize I was awake. "May I have some water?"

They both turned to me.

"Of course you can," Mom said, walking over to me.

"I better get back down to Hope. Tanya, stay strong." He turned and left.

"If you wake up later and I am not here, I will just be down seeing your sister; I will be back shortly."

"Okay." I wanted to see Hope myself, but I knew that I could not.

The next time I woke up, the nurse was changing my IV's. Mom was by the window; she came over when she saw my eyes. "You have been out for a while; they are starting the transplant."

I smiled at her, and closed my eyes. By the third day after the transplant, I was feeling much better. Instead of sleeping all the time with brief bits of being awake, I was up most of the day and took a few naps. I was still in isolation, so I spent time watching TV or reading.

"Mom, if you want to go home for a bit, I will be okay."

"I know you will, but not until after you are out of isolation."

"What about school?"

"Tanya, you have a few other things to worry about."

"So?"

"Hope and Sara are returning on Monday; Kate is taking them. When you are better, I will enroll you in the same school Elizabeth goes to."

"No, I want to go back to my school."

"I know you do, but you are going to be in the hospital for a while, then you will be at home for a while. School is still a ways down the list."

"Well, I have a lot of free time on my hands, so you can get me my homework, and then Hope or Sara can turn it in for me. Then I will not fall behind."

"We will see."

Three days later, I was released from isolation. Kate, Ann, and Elizabeth were all there to see me. Hope and Sara had already started back at school. They stayed for about two hours. Mom was true to her word. She started going home at night, but she always returned first thing in the morning, usually with a gift for me. On day five in my normal room, the doctor came in to see me.

"Well, Tanya, are you sick of the hospital yet?"

"Yes."

"Would you like your own room better?"

"Yes."

"Would you like to sleep in your own bed this afternoon?"

"Are you serious?"

"Yes, your mother is signing your release papers right now."

Just then the door opened, and mom appeared, smiling. The doctor removed the last IV I had. "Why don't you change; I will go send a nurse up to wheel you out of here."

"Thank you."

"Mrs. Delecroie, if her temp goes above 100°, bring her back. And Tanya, just because you are going home, do not think you are cured. You get home and go to bed. No outside activities; you have a checkup in one week. We will see then."

"Okay." He left. Mom handed me a pair of jeans and a sweatshirt. By the time I was finished changing, the nurse was there with the wheelchair. I was on my way back to the penthouse.

"Welcome home, Tanya. Now go change and get into bed."

"But I just got here."

"Yes, and you are still under doctor's orders, so to your bed."

I went to my room, and a new pile of movies was on my TV, a stack of books on my nightstand, and on my desk were my schoolbooks! And a list of assignments. Laying on my bed was a new pair of pajamas; I changed into them and started looking through the books when Mom showed up.

"Thank you!"

"For what?"

"The books! My school things."

"Oh, that. Now listen, if I catch you overdoing it, I will take them away, and you will be going to school here with Elizabeth."

I smiled at her. "Thank you."

"You are welcome. Why don't you take a nap, and then I will get lunch for you?"

"May I eat in the dining room?"

"Yes, you may."

I crawled into bed; she gave me a kiss and left the room. Just after 4 p.m., Elizabeth showed up. I was in the den playing a board game with Mom.

"Tanya, you are home!"

"Yes, they released me this morning."

"That is great!"

"Elizabeth, she is still under strict orders to rest and is not allowed out of this apartment, so do not let her fool you."

"Yes, I am sure she needs it."

"She does."

"She is sitting right here."

"Yes, she is, and she also needs to go rest before dinner, so up to your room."

"I am not tired."

"So go get in bed and read a book, no homework."

"Okay." I got up and walked back to my room.

The week continued. I ate all of my meals in the dining room and worked on some homework after breakfast. After lunch I would take a nap, then play a game with Mom. Before dinner I would read my book. After dinner I would watch some TV and get ready for bed. Kate, Ann, and Elizabeth all kept me company. When the week was over, I returned to the doctor.

"Tanya, the bad news is that you are not invincible. The good news: You are in remission!"

Mom and I hugged.

"So this means I can go back to my old life?"

"Soon, with some restrictions. Wait another week before you go back to school. Take your medicine every day. And lots of rest. Your immune system is still weak."

Mom took me out to lunch to celebrate. "Your father is not going to approve of the jeans if you are to go back to your normal life."

I looked down at what I was wearing. "I guess it is worth it."

"So do I. Now, I only have seven days before I lose you back to school, so you and I are spending time together."

She was not lying. That week she took me to shows and out shopping. We went to Ellis Island and to the Statue of Liberty. We went on a carriage ride through Central Park. Craig was in and out. Elizabeth joined us when she could. On Saturday, we had a family lunch, minus Hope and Sara.

Chapter Nine

Sunday Mom took me back to school. I am not sure who was more excited, my sisters or me. School kept me busy. Since Mom had let me stay up to date with the work, I was officially caught up. I had some new classes including French. I had no interest in learning French; however, Craig was determined that we all would learn French. I did not pay much attention in the class.

My second week back, Mom called and said that she would be taking us back to New York for the weekend, and we needed to get our homework through Tuesday.

"Why?"

"Tanya, do you always have to have a reason?"

"Yes."

She started laughing. "Well, at least you are honest."

"So why?"

"You have a checkup on Tuesday morning."

"For what?"

"Do you not remember how sick you were just a few weeks ago?"

"I am fine now."

"Yes, and we are going to make sure that you stay that way."

"All right."

"I will be there in two hours; see you then, baby. I love you."

"Love you too." I hung up the phone. Hope and Sara were in the library, so I decided to give the Johnsons a call.

"Hello?"

"Hi!"

"Tanya! We were getting worried about you; we have not heard from you since New Years."

"I know, I am sorry. I have been busy."

"You are doing okay?"

"Yes."

"So how is school?"

"Fine. I am taking two days off and going back to New York."

"Why?"

"Some celebration or something."

"Oh."

"Is Sam home?"

"No, she is still at school."

"Oh yeah, time change. Will you tell her I called?"

"I will."

"I have to go. Talk to you later."

"Goodbye. I love you."

I hung up the phone. I felt odd talking to her now, even more since I did not want them to know about my leukemia.

I found Hope and Sara. We went and saw our teachers, then returned to our room forty-five minutes before Mom was going to arrive. Mr. Martin, our French teacher, requested a meeting with her when she got here. He said that he would give her our assignments. We told her, so when she arrived, she went to see him and then we left.

Dinner was waiting when we arrived at the penthouse. Ann, Kate, and Elizabeth were all at the table. After we ate, we all excused ourselves to the den.

"Tanya, hold on."

I shrugged and turned to the others. "I will be in in a moment." They all left.

"Tanya, sit down." I sat back down in my chair. "The reason Mr. Martin wanted to speak with me was because of you."

"Oh."

"Do you have anything else to say?"

"I do not like French."

"I do not like you going to boarding school, but I deal with it."

"That is different."

"Even if it is, not liking French is no excuse. You will pay attention in class, you will get an A, and you will learn to accept the class. Do you understand?"

"Yeah."

"Listen, I know you have been under a lot of stress, but you are the one who said you wanted to go back to normal."

"I know."

"Let me have your cell phone and your debit card please." I got them out and handed them to her. "You are grounded until further notice."

"And that changes my life how?"

"Being smart is not going to get you out of trouble."

"Sorry."

"Tonight, you are on your way to bed, then tomorrow you are doing your French homework before anything else."

"Okay."

"Now, come give me a hug."

I got up and gave her a hug, then she slipped her hand on my forehead. "Mom."

"Hey, I have not asked you once tonight how you are feeling; as your mother, I am allowed to check, and you are a bit warm."

"I am fine, and I am on my way to bed."

"Goodnight. I love you."

"Love you too."

"Tanya, is your French done?"

"Yeah."

"Let me see it, your homework please."

I went to my desk and pulled it out, then handed it to her.

"This is acceptable—however, not you're best. If Mr. Martin tells me again that you are not paying attention in his class, you will be back here enjoying la home school."

"Okay."

"Okay? Are you feeling all right?"

"Yes, I am fine."

She gave me a curious look, then smiled at me. "You are grounded, so today I have a few errands. You are coming with me."

"What about Hope and Sara?"

"They are going with Ann—shopping, then to dinner."

"Oh."

"Go get your hat and coat, also your gloves and your scarf. It is cold out."

"But."

"Tanya, it is cold, and your immune system is still weak. You can worry about being normal; I will worry about your health."

"It is not that cold."

"Cold enough, and if you keep complaining, you will not have to worry about being pulled out of school, if you catch my drift."

I looked at her, then turned to get my coat. The coat was long navy blue wool; it had buttons down the front. The scarf, hat, and gloves were all lavender. When I returned, she smiled then wrapped the scarf around my neck. "There, now don't you look adorable?"

"I do not want to look adorable, that is for babies."

"Fine, you look like a very pretty young lady. Now let's get going."

We went to her attorney's, then her accountant's. It was two hours later when she was done. I was bored. She decided from there we would take a cab rather than walk. When we got it, I was expecting her to give the address of the penthouse, but she gave one that I was not familiar with.

"Where are we going?"

"To my designers. I have to see the designs for some of your sisters' and your spring outfits."

"Designers? I thought you just bought them."

"Some things, I call my sales girl and tell her what I need; the rest I have designed."

When she was done, we were both hungry. She took me to a French restaurant. By the time dessert came, I was very tired.

"Baby, are you all right?"

"Yeah, just tired."

She reached over and put her hand on my forehead. "Tanya, you have a fever."

"I am fine."

"You are not; I should not have had you outside so long today."

"Mom, really, I am fine."

She ignored my statement and called for the limo; then she called Craig.

"Tanya is burning up. I am taking her to the hospital."

"I am fine." She still ignored me.

"Okay, we will see you in a few hours; I will call when I know what is wrong." She hung up the phone, stood up, took my hand, and we left the restaurant. The limo was waiting outside.

"I do not need to go to the hospital."

"We will let the doctor decide."

When we arrived at the hospital, they took me into a room and started taking my vitals. "Temp is 102."

"She had a bone marrow transplant about five weeks ago."

The nurse and doctor looked at each other, then asked Mom to join them outside. They returned a few moments later.

"Tanya, they are going to run a few tests and give you something to bring down your fever."

"I do not want tests; I want to go home."

"We will see, sweetie."

The nurse came back. "Tanya, we are going to need you to change into this gown and get into the bed."

"Mom."

"Tanya, please, I will make this up to you."

I changed and sat down on the bed. The nurse hooked up an IV. Then she drew some blood.

"Tanya, this last shot is going to make you tired."

It did, and I fell asleep. When I woke up it was dark; I was in a different room. Craig and Mom were both asleep on the sofa by the window. I got out of bed and went into the bathroom; I was used to taking the IV stand with me.

"Tanya, what are you doing?"

"I had to use the bathroom."

"Thank god. I woke up and your bed was empty." She helped me back into the bed, then I fell asleep again.

"Good morning! Tanya, how are you feeling?"

"Fine. Can I go home now?"

"We will see what the doctor says."

Craig looked from me to Mom. "I will go find him." He left; Mom came over and handed me some jeans and a sweatshirt.

"I had this brought over for you; do you want to change?"

"So I am going home?"

"We'll see." I changed, then Craig returned with the doctor.

"Mr. and Mrs. Delecroie, none of our tests show any thing indicating that her leukemia is back; the fever is strictly from the flu. You will want a checkup with her normal doctor just to be on the safe side."

"She already has one on Tuesday."

"Good, well, until then, lots of rest and fluids. You can take her home."

"Thank you. Can we go now?'

"All right, hold on just a moment. Your father and I have to go sign your release papers." They returned about 10 minutes later; Mom handed me my coat.

"Tanya, bed now."

"But I am not tired."

"You still have a fever of 101; you need rest."

"Mom."

"Sweetie, please just listen to your father. Read a book or something, but go lie down."

"Fine." I turned to leave, but Hope passed me in the door.

"Mom, I don't feel well."

Mom looked from me over to Hope; then she felt Hope's forehead.

"My god, you are burning up also; go sit on the couch."

Hope and I both sat on the couch, and Mom returned to take her temp. "102. All right, you two stay here. I am going to go check on Sara and Elizabeth. I have never had two kids get sick and the rest not follow." She turned and left again.

Hope and I stretched out on the couch with our heads at opposite ends.

"Turn on the TV."

"You have the remote."

"Oh, what do you want to watch?"

"I do not care. Where is Sara?"

"She was still in bed."

"Oh."

Mom came back in. "Well, at least Elizabeth is not ill. Three out of four, great."

"Sara's sick too?"

"Yes, she is in bed. Now, you two go find your beds. I will be up to see you and bring you all some juice soon." We both got up and walked out. I reached my bed and fell back asleep.

Mom's hand was on my forehead when I woke up. "Good afternoon, sleepyhead."

"Hi."

"Your fever seems to be down a bit." She took my temp. "100, that is an improvement."

"How are Hope and Sara?"

"Sleeping. I am going to make you some soup. Any kind you want?"

"Toast and butter."

She smiled at me, then walked over to my desk. "I knew you were going to ask for that."

"Thanks," I said as she handed me the plate.

"Tanya, we need to make a deal. You need to tell me when you are not feeling well, and I promise not to overreact every time and take you to the hospital. Deal?"

"Okay."

The next two days, she kept us all inside. She rented us videos to watch and let us take over the den. On Tuesday morning, my fever was gone; after breakfast, Mom took me back to the doctor.

"I see you were in the hospital for a fever of 102?"

"Yes, I overreacted. She came down with the flu first, but actually, all of the triplets have been sick with the flu."

"Well, we can never be too careful. I will run some tests just to be sure, but like you said, if her sisters had the flu also, she is almost guaranteed to get it with her weak immune system."

The doctor confirmed that I was still in remission and just had the flu. Mom decided that we were not going to return to school as planned; she wanted to make sure all of us were better, so we stayed in New York until Thursday.

I did start paying attention in French. I wanted to get ungrounded, but I also wanted to keep my 4.0. I talked to Mom every other day. The snow finally started to melt, and the weather warmed up a bit. Our spring break was coming up just around the corner. I joined the field hockey team for the spring. I wanted to play soccer, but that was only in the fall here. I had never played before, but I was having fun! Mom was nervous about it, but my doctor said it would be good for me.

On the day of our first game, we all wore our team uniforms instead of the school uniform.

"Tanya, are you excited?"

"More nervous than anything."

"How can you be nervous? You have spent more time out there playing than you have with us."

"I know, but it is the butterfly thing. I have to go; we have a meeting before the match."

"Okay, good luck."

"Thanks, Sara."

An hour later, the stands filled, and the game began. I scored once; my team made a total of three goals. The other team lost by one. When we cleared the field, I ran over to get my water bottle. Mom was holding it.

"What are you doing here?"

"I postponed my meeting; I could not miss your first field hockey game."

"Oh."

"I see you are also my athlete. Not only good at soccer, but this too."

"I have been practicing."

"I can see that. Why don't we go out for dinner to celebrate?"

"I still have homework."

"You can bring it with you."

Dinner was good; we discussed our plans for our spring break. Mom wanted to take us to Germany since Craig was going to be there on business. But as I had already learned, things do not always go as planned.

Chapter Ten

On Thursday afternoon, there was a school assembly; Hope, Sara, and I were all going to be given awards for bring in the National Junior Honor Society. Mom and Craig were both coming to see it; afterward, our spring vacation would begin, and we were going to Germany. Off for eleven days! Thursday morning, Hope and Sara both woke up with red dots covering them; it turned out to be the chicken pox. Our room was quarantined. I was not allowed back in there. Craig ended up having to fly out early to Germany on an emergency; he was gone by the time the school called Mom. We had lunch together, and then I went back to my classes. Just before JPD, I was called into the office.

"Miss Delecroie, your mother wishes to speak to you. She is waiting for you in the commons of your dorm."

"Thank you, Mrs. Winterhaven."

I turned and walked out of the office. "Mom, what is up? Why did you call me out of class?"

"I know you love that class, but I need to talk to you. About spring break, with your sisters sick, I am going to be focusing my attention on them. I do not want you at the penthouse; your immune system should not take another shock, and you have not had them yet. You would find it to hard to stay away from them. Your father is in Germany already, Kate and William are in Brazil, and Ann is in LA, but she is getting ready to go to Australia."

"You are leaving me here?"

"No, I was thinking about letting you go to the Johnsons for the break."

"What!"

"It is that or I send you to Germany to be with your father."

"No, I would love to go see the Johnsons."

"Well, I have a plane ticket for you, but the flight leaves in two hours, so you are going to miss the awards."

"That is okay. I am flying on an airline?"

"Yes, your father took one plane to Germany, and I need the other to get your sister out of here."

Mom took me to the airport, got me checked in, and waited with me until the plane left. I was in first class, had a layover in Chicago, then on to Sacramento where they were going to pick me up and drive me to Waterford.

When I got off of the plane, they were all waiting for me. I ran and gave them all a hug.

"Tanya, you look so different, so grown up in that uniform. How do you like the school?"

"I love it! I am on the field hockey team now."

"We are glad that you could come see us. I was so surprised when Kerstin Delecroie called. Let's get your bags and go home."

Sam made fun of me for having luggage with my initials embroidered into it, and also about my uniform. My bed was still in Sam's room, but it was covered in all of her junk. I was tired when we got there, so I went straight to bed. Sam's alarm woke me up in the morning. She still had to go to school; I went down to breakfast with her.

"Tanya, we were not planning on having you come to visit. Sam has to go to school, your dad has to go to work, I am taking Isabelle to daycare, then going into the office; would you mind being dragged along with me?"

"Actually, could I go to school? I would like to see some of my friends."

"Let me call the school to make sure." She returned a few minutes later to say it was all set up; in addition, I was going to go to all of Keri's classes, and Keri did not know! I ran upstairs, changed into one of my jumpers, braided my hair, then took my laptop and some of my books and put them into my backpack. I thought I should take some work with me since I was not actually going to be participating in the classes. I also grabbed $20 of the $500 Mom had given me to bring.

Sam and I walked to the school I had once attended; classes were just beginning when I got there. Mrs. Smith, the secretary, took me down to Keri's first class. I walked in and said hello; she looked up, then took a second glance.

"Tanya, you are back!"

"Hi, Keri!"

"Look at you, you really do look so different! Are you back for good?"

"No, I am just here for a week; I am on spring break. Mom arranged it for me to come back here."

"Mom? You call her Mom?"

"Yes, she is. Anyways, Craig is in Germany, my sisters both have the chicken pox, and Mom decided I would be bored, so here I am! How are you?"

"Okay."

"All right, class, I know you are all excited to see Tanya, so Tanya, why don't you come up here and tell everyone what you have been up to this past year?"

"All right." I walked to the front of the class. "As you all know, after school got out last year, I went to live with my biological family. My life has changed a whole lot since then. I spend my time divided between four places. My parents own an estate in London and outside of LA; they also have a penthouse in New York City. I also live in a dorm at the school I attend called the Buchanan Academy."

"Wow, you actually go to boarding school? How did you face that?"

"I actually asked to go there; my sisters—oh yeah, I am a triplet—they attend this school. I went there last year, and I was impressed, so I asked to go."

"What is New York City like?"

"Very different from here. It is really big! There is so much to do; I am actually going there next Thursday."

"If you could come back here like nothing happened, would you?"

"I love my family and friends I have here, but I also love the family I have there. Eight months ago, I would have begged to come back here; however, now I don't think I could. I now have two families."

By second period, everyone was getting back into his or her studies. I sat in the back and played on my laptop. I was not in the mood to do my work. When the day was over, I was ready to go home. Keri and I did have fun for the most part. I walked with Keri, just like old times. That night we went to my favorite pizza place for dinner.

Sam and I went to the mall on Saturday. I had bought a few things at the different stores, but then when I was looking at a pair of jeans in a designer store, Sam started in on me.

"Tanya, you cannot buy those; they are too expensive."

"Yes, I can; do you want a pair?"

"I can get five pairs of jeans at Sam's World for $75. Besides, where are you going to get another $150?"

"I have $400 cash left; otherwise, I can put it on my credit card."

"You have a credit card? Do you know how many times I have to babysit to get cash like that?"

"Yes, Sam, I do, but what's the problem? My parents are rich, so I get money to spend. If I have it, I am not sure what the problem is; I am offering to buy you the same."

"Your parents? Whatever. OUR parents will have a fit when they hear how much you paid for those."

"Tell them. It is not that big a deal. Heck, each one of my school uniforms cost $300, and I have nine of those, not to mention the rest of my clothes. Mom gets some of them from a designer."

"Whatever. Just buy them if you must." I did, which then made her mad at me for the rest of the afternoon. When we got back to their house, I started on my homework. I heard the phone ring.

"Tanya, it is for you."

I picked up the phone.

"Hi, sweetie, how are you?"

"Good, how are Hope and Sara?"

"They are doing okay. They are not too happy having to stay inside all day. I think I have bought them the entire video store."

"More than you bought me?"

"Yes. They are awake all day, just uncomfortable; you slept most of the time."

"I guess that gives them something to do."

"Baby, are you all right?"

"Yes, I am just working on my homework."

"Are you sure?"

"Yes, Mom, everything is great!"

"All right, so what have you been doing?"

"Yesterday I went to my old school and hung out with my old friends, then today we went shopping at the mall."

"Well, just remember if you run out of cash that you have your credit card."

"I know, but there really is not a whole lot to buy around here."

"Well, I better let you get back to your homework. Your sisters are finally sleeping soundly. Otherwise I would let you talk to them."

"That is okay. Tell them I hope they feel better."

"I will. I love you, baby."

"Love you too." I hung up the phone and turned around. Sam was sitting there.

"So, there is not too much to buy here?"

"She told me to use my credit cards if I ran out of money. I was telling her I would not."

"You have turned into a spoiled brat over the past year. I am not sure where the little sister I had went when she left last year."

"It is not my fault that I have money, and you are just jealous." She was acting like a snob. I was trying to be nice and offering to buy things for her, and then she had the nerve to call me a spoiled brat. She glared at me, then turned and left the room. I went to bed early that night. Sunday morning, we did not speak to each other.

"Tanya, this is your day, whatever you want to do. Sam is going back to school tomorrow, and your dad will have to go back to work, so today it is whatever you like."

"I don't care; anything would be fine."

"What would you really like to do?"

"Well, I have not been to the beach recently."

"All right, so we will drive to the ocean. You girls better go get dressed!"

I ran upstairs and changed into a sundress, then I got out my bathing suit. Sam was going to have a fit when she saw it. This one was new, and I had not seen it before. It was a purple polo suit. I also took out my cover-up and headed downstairs. Sam was down there complaining.

"I do not see why we have to spend the day at the beach; it is such a long drive. Isabelle is not good in the car."

"Sam, your sister wants to go to the beach, and Isabelle is fine in the car; she will sleep half the way, anyways."

"She is not my sister."

"Yes, she is. She is just as much our daughter as you and Isabelle, even if she does not live here anymore."

"Whatever."

I looked at Sam and gave her the same look that she gave me. Then I looked back up. "If Sam would rather go to a movie or something, that would be all right. Not very original, but it would be okay." I knew that was going to set her off.

"Not very original? I bet you go see all of the movies when they come out, don't you?"

"I do not need to; we have a theater in the manor. Mom said that one day she will take me to a premier; however, there has not been anything I am interested in yet."

"I told you, you are just a SB now."

"Hold it, you two. Samantha, why are you calling Tanya an SB? What is it?"

"She has turned into a spoiled brat, and she is rubbing it into everyone's face."

"She is not a spoiled brat, and I think she is handling herself quite well for everything she has gone through. Now, apologize and get your things; we are leaving in a 10 minutes." Sam stared at me, then got up and walked out of the room.

The drive was long; Sam and I were in the back, separated by Isabelle. We ate lunch at a beach-side café, then spent the next few hours running around on the beach. Isabelle and I played some games and went into the water. Sam and I did not say a word to each other. When we got home, I went straight to bed.

I ignored Sam when she got up for school in the morning. After she left, I got up and got ready. I went with Liz to her office; then we went shopping. When we were done, we picked up Isabelle from day care. She showed me all of the pictures she had drawn. We picked Sam up from her school.

"Sam, I need you to babysit on Friday."

"Mom, I told you I am not going to be a built-in babysitter; I have things to do. I don't need to spend my time with the kid because you decided to adopt a four-year-old."

I saw Liz open her mouth, but I jumped in. "You have the nerve to call me a spoiled brat? I went from having to share everything with you to sharing everything with my two sisters. I may be spoiled, but you, dear Sam, are the brat. You are the one acting like your world is coming to an end just because you are asked to babysit in five days. That is advanced notice. I don't even get that when we fly across the country."

They all just looked at me. Sam was the brat; she no longer had to share with me, Isabelle was too young to share with, she had her own room, and she was ungrateful.

"You, Tanya, do not know what you are talking about. I am the one that has had to put up with never getting away from you, and your picture is everywhere. You were on the cover of *People Magazine* not once, but twice! Mom keeps telling me how Mrs. Delecroie sends her letters of your progress. You used to call me all the time; NOW you hardly ever call! I have to keep asking MOM if she got a letter from Mrs. Delecroie."

"My mom sends you letters about my progress?"

"Every month, she sends me an update. I was really upset when you were in that coma last fall; she called us whenever there was a change."

"I want to call my mom." Sam gave me a snooty look. I went over, picked up the phone, and dialed the number for the penthouse. Mom answered it. "Hi, Mom."

"Tanya, what is the matter?"

"Nothing, I just wanted to talk. I did not wake you, did I?"

"No, Elizabeth and I went to a show. How is California?"

"Fine. Sam told me about the letters."

"Oh, I see. Well, I know that when you were gone, I would have liked some information on how you were doing. I thought they might as well."

"Thank you. You did not tell them about the…"

"No, I did not; Tanya, is it about 10 p.m.?"

"Yes."

"Well, I think you should be on your way to bed."

"Okay, see you in a few days."

"Yes, I will pick you up at the airport on Thursday. I love you."

"Love you too." I hung up the phone and went to bed.

The next morning, everyone went to work and school. I stayed at the house and worked on the paper I had; Wednesday, I worked on my presentation.

Wednesday evening, we drove to Sacramento. I treated everyone to dinner, then we stayed in a hotel that night. My flight was early. They left after I was checked in and with the airline agent. This time I was on a direct flight to LGA, in first class, of course. I arrived in New York at 4 p.m. Mom was waiting at the gate for me, and I ran to her and gave her a hug.

"I think I like this kind of homecoming; what has gotten into you?"

"Nothing, I just missed everyone."

"Well, why don't we get you home so you can see your sisters? They are much better, but are not happy about spending the first half of their break being sick in bed. You will have to talk to them. You all still have a week left, so we need to do something special." She put her arm around me, and we headed back to the penthouse.

Hope and Sara were waiting for me, and we all hugged. "We want to go to Hawaii, but you get a vote."

"That is fine with me!"

"Good," Mom agreed. Elizabeth was also going to go with us; she had the one week off, and it was the same as our second week. Friday night, we went out to a show and dinner. Hope and Sara were excited about leaving the apartment. I had to laughed at them. I remembered feeling the same way. Craig returned from Germany Saturday morning.

Saturday afternoon, we boarded the plane for Hawaii! Mom made us work on our homework for the first part of the flight, but she let us quit when she saw we were bored and playing around.

"Tanya, come here please." She patted the seat next to her on the couch. I sat down and looked at her quizzically. She brushed my hair back behind my ear. "Are you okay?"

"Yeah, I am fine."

"I was worried when you came home; you have not been yourself. You are quiet and keeping to yourself; I know something is wrong, so what is it?"

"It is nothing, trust me."

"Something happened at the Johnsons."

I looked away from her because I did not want her to see my face.

She started rubbing my back. "This is a long flight, and we are not moving until you tell me what it is."

"Sam is blaming me; she called me a spoiled brat."

"What?"

"We started yelling at each other, then stopped speaking. She said that I did not care about them anymore, and I was rubbing my wealth in her face. The only thing I did was offer to buy her something. Then she was on my case because I stopped calling her all the time. I couldn't call her; it was not possible."

"Did you tell her the reason why you did not call for so long?"

"No, I did not want her to feel sorry for me; she would feel guilty for everything she said."

"When you were kidnapped, Kate was mad at you for leaving. Annie tried everything she could think of to get her to come around. She realized that she was mad at herself; she blamed herself for your disappearance. It was a very rough time for her; I am sure that Sam is going through the same thing. She is probably upset that you are not with her anymore, mad at herself for being mad at you."

"Why won't she answer me?"

Craig put down his paper and looked at me. "Tanya." He handed me his cell phone. "Try calling her."

I looked at him, a little shocked; this was the first time that he was actually doing something for me that I could tell. I took the phone and dialed. Sam answered.

"Sam, it is me."

"Oh, hi. I really don't have time to talk. What do you need?"

"I just wanted to talk to you; did you get my email?"

"Yeah, what about it?"

"How are things going?"

"Fine. I have to go." She hung up the phone.

I handed the phone back to Craig, tears started rolling down my cheeks, and Mom pulled me closer to her.

"I am sure she is just upset." Craig moved over to me. "You have five other sisters that would do anything for you. When she comes around, she will know where you are; until then, you have your sisters here."

Hope moved to sit on the other side of me. "Tanya, are you okay?" I nodded my head, and Craig moved back to his chair. Mom looked at me.

"She is just having a hard time dealing with a few things about Sam."

"Oh, well, if there is anything we can do, just let us know. Sara and I are always here for you."

"I know, Hope, and I do not have to tell you; you just know, same way I do when you or Sara need something." We started laughing, and Mom squeezed us both close to her, giving us both a hug. I was caught in the middle. Sara came over and joined in; I was cheered up instantly.

"That's my girls."

Craig reserved the presidential suite for us; it was about the same size as the penthouse. Kate and Ann were going to fly in later to meet us. Sara and I were going to share a room; Hope and Elizabeth were going to share another.

"Girls, I know you are going to want to have fun, but there are ground rules."

"Mom, we are on vacation!"

"I know, and I want you to return from vacation. So you are not to go to the beach or leave the hotel without one of your sisters or your father and I."

"That is easy, we always go places together."

"Hope, you know that I mean—one of your older sisters. You may go to the hotel pool with each other, but you have to tell me you are going there."

"Okay, we can live with that."

Chapter Eleven

When we returned to school, our room had been cleaned from top to bottom. My uniforms had all been cleaned and pressed; I also had some spring uniforms, vests, and short-sleeve shirts. I talked to some of my friends in the common room before going up and to bed. My first spring break from the Buchanan Academy for girls was over, school would be done in two months, and that would mark my one-year anniversary of when I had come back to this family, my family. I had my hands full when school resumed. I was beat by the end of the day, Field Hockey was well underway, and in classes, we were preparing for the end of the year. This year, we were going to take a series of test that would indicate where we should focus our studies over the next few years. Mom and I stuck to our deal: I dealt with being normal and having fun, and she dealt with my medical issues. She let me do almost anything as long as I did not complain and let her watch my health. We all got into a routine. Hope, Sara, and I always had dinner together. I talked to my mom every other day. I, however, had not talked to the Johnsons since I last talked to Sam on the plane.

Mom and Craig arrived and said that they had conferences with our teachers. We had the day off so all the teachers could meet with the parents.

I spent the morning working on my homework; we were going to New York for the weekend. Before my field hockey game, I changed into my uniform.

Hope and Sara brought up a tray of food. "We thought you might want something to eat."

"Thank you! I am starving." I ate, then ran out to the field for the game. I scored three out of the four times we did; we won the game!

"Good game! Baby, your sisters said that you finished your homework, so we're going straight to the car."

Two hours later, we arrived at the penthouse.

"Tanya, go clean up, then meet us for dinner; it will be served in twenty minutes."

I headed up to my room, but I stopped and stuck my head in Elizabeth's room. "Hey, Liz, how is Snowball?"

"Good, he is on your bed last I saw."

Twenty minutes later, I was changed and being served dinner.

"Girls, as you know, we had a conference with your teachers today; after dinner, I want a meeting with each of you. First Tanya, then Sara, and finally, Hope."

"Yes, sir," we answered in unison. We were all quiet for the remainder of dinner. Craig got up and walked out when we were done. I sat in my seat, not wanting to move.

Mom came over and took my hand. "Let's go." We went into his office, Mom and I sat on the couch, and he closed the door and sat across from us in a chair.

"Tanya, we have told you what we expect from your grades and your education, correct?"

"Yes, sir."

"And you know what is expected from you?"

"Yes, sir."

"Good." He opened a file. "This is a file on your entire education. To tell you the truth, I was worried about sending you to this school; it is a prep school with very high standards. The previous school you went to was a substandard public school."

"Substandard?"

"Yes. However, you have really surprised me. With everything you have gone through this year, you have missed so much school, and you still surpassed our expectations. You are currently ranked number one in your class."

"I am?"

"Yes, you are, plus you are a star athlete. We are very proud of you."

"Does that mean I am ungrounded?"

"Yes, baby."

"Tanya, there is more to it. You have missed half the school year. What are you going to do when you are there the entire time without the hospital breaks?"

"What do you mean?"

"You did your homework in half the time it took your sisters. I think we should look into something that will stimulate your mind more."

"I have my hands full already; I cannot handle any more work."

"We are thinking more of another school."

"Change schools again? NO, we all love it here."

"Your mother and I have been discussing this; we believe you will benefit from this school, and it is in LA, so you could live at home."

"And Hope and Sara?"

"They can choose if they want to stay or change."

"You want me to go to a school where everyone is a geek?"

"No, they are not all geeks."

"I want to stay."

"Baby, we want what is best for you."

Craig was silent. Then he looked at me for a moment. "Give it a try. If you do not like it, we will let you change schools again. Your mother and I want what is best for you. Mrs. Winterhaven already sent your file over to this school; you were accepted to begin in the fall."

I looked at him and shook my head. "Thank you, Dad, thank you for listening to me." He got up and gave me a hug. "May I go upstairs now?"

"You do not want to stay and tell your sisters?"

"No, I will pass. Hope is going to be upset."

"All right, you may go."

A half hour later, Sara came into my room. "Hope is very upset."

"I figured."

"Mom said you were not too happy either."

"No, I am not; I do not want to change schools again."

"She will get over it. Dad has just always told her she should be the best, and she is the older triplet."

"That is not right; she has to figure it out."

Mom stuck her head in the door. "Sara, you need to go get ready for bed, and I will be in shortly."

Sara left, then Mom sat down on my bed. "We know you are not happy about this. Sara and Hope both said they would go where you go. Tanya, I know you are only 13, but you need to start thinking about your future. Kate is a lawyer, and Ann is a doctor. Those are both excellent careers. You should consider one of them."

"I am only 13."

"I know, just think about it." She kissed me and left.

We returned to school on Monday. We had four weeks left before the term was going to be over. When Mom left, I went into Hope's room.

"All right, we have to figure out something to stay here."

"You do not want to go?"

"Heck no, I will go nuts! Are you going to help me?"

"Do you have to ask?"

"Ask for what?"

"Sara, we want to stay. Are you in?"

"I am in whereever you two are!"

"So let's call Mom and tell her we don't want to leave this school."

"Mrs. Winterhaven is the person who helped Mom decided."

"No, okay." Hope paused. "So we will have to go to a new school, for Mom will not back down; she wants all of us to get the best education. Let's do our research on this place."

For the next three weeks, we worked with our heads together trying to come up with some idea; nothing panned out. We pulled up the information on the school she was talking about: Pavilion. Hope and Sara would then go to St. Margaret's. We wanted everything to be planned out before we took our case to Mom and Dad; we wanted nothing for them to say no to. We finally found the school we were looking for. It was located outside of LA and had two levels of programs. The week before our exams, we went back to New York with a mission. After dinner, we requested their presence in the den.

"We ask that you please let us finish, and please listen to what we have to say."

"Hope, what is all of this about?"

"Craig, I am sure if we listen, they will tell us."

"Thank you. Sara, Tanya, and I know that you want us to be healthy, well educated, and happy. We also understand the school will no longer provide us all with an education to challenge us. We do not want to be separated; we feel that this will interfere with our happiness and then, in turn, our health. We have discussed it and have developed an additional idea, one that will give us all the education to challenge us and keep us together. In addition, the school we have chosen is in LA, so we could live at home." Sara and I handed them the information about Premier.

They looked at each other and then at the materials we gave them. "Girls, please excuse us."

We left them alone and went into the living room. After about an hour, they came out and looked at us. "You all really want this?"

"Yes."

"Enough to live with us year round? Willingly?"

"Yes."

"All right, you may all attend the Premier Academy starting in the fall."

We all jumped up and gave them a hug. "Thank you!"

"You are welcome. I called the school, they have agreed to accept all three of you, and we had better not disappoint them, so go study for your exams."

I went to my room and decided to call the Johnsons.

"Tanya, we have not heard from you in a while."

"I talked to Sam; she wanted nothing to do with me. I decided I should steer clear."

"I wish you would not."

"I am finishing up with school this week, then we are moving back to California."

"For the summer?"

"No, for a while. We are going to start a school there, live at home."

"Oh, so they want to spend some more time with you?"

"Please do not start. They are very good to me."

"Tanya, I just do not think that they have your best interest in mind."

"You are wrong, all they want is the best for me. Sorry, I have to go; we are on our way out the door." I hung up before she had a chance to say anything else.

"I did not mean to listen."

I turned my head. "Mom, I did not see you there."

"Tanya, I have not seen you talk to the Johnsons in a while. I knew you were having problems with Sam; are you also with Liz?"

"I do not want to talk about it."

"Okay, but if you do, I am here."

"I know."

"Are you ready for your exams?"

"Yes."

"Good. Would you like to do anything special? When I pick you up on Friday, we are going back to LA."

"I guess I would like to see a show or something."

"That sounds good to me. Tomorrow, dinner and a show."

Mom told Mrs. Winterhaven her decision and said she would have our room cleaned out by Friday evening. The word spread fast that we would not be returning, but it did not hit me until we drove away Friday afternoon.

My room was the same, everything in its place.

"You are going to spend a lot more time here."

"What?"

"No more boarding school, coming home every day. I will get to see you all of the time!"

"Do I have time to reconsider boarding school in Switzerland?" I said, smiling.

"I believe I can arrange a nice tutor to come into the house."

"NO!"

"All right, why don't you go get ready for bed."

"It is only 8 p.m."

"But it is 11 p.m. in New York, the time your body is running on."

I got up early and went out to see my horse; everyone was up when I got back to the house.

"Tanya, you were up early."

"You made me go to bed early, so I go up early."

"I think I am interviewing tutors this morning."

"Are you always going to use that as a threat?"

"Probably," she said, smiling, then gave me a hug.

"Mom?"

"Yes, baby?"

"Keri, can she come visit for a few days?"

"You are still speaking to her?"

"Yes, we email all the time."

"Oh, that is good. Give me her number and I will call her mother."

"Thanks, Mom."

"You are welcome. By the way you are starting your summer schedule on Monday."

"Mom, why can we not just be bored for a while?"

"Riding, piano, and trumpet. The rest of the time is yours."

"Okay, I am going to change." I changed, then I emailed Keri and told her that my mom would be calling hers. She was online so we started instant messaging. I lost track of time, and an hour later, I sat down on the couch with a book.

A hand was on my head. Even before opening my eyes, I stated, "I am fine, Mom."

"You are sleeping in the middle of the morning."

"I got up early."

"I have to go run some errands, and you are coming with me."

"Do I have to?"

"Yes, now let's get going." I got up and followed her out of my room. We went to her travel agent, and she set up a flight for Keri, then we went to lunch. Then we went to an office building.

"What is this place?"

"A doctors office."

"MOM!"

"Well, I did not think you wanted to fly to New York City for every visit. I called here, they wanted to see you, and then you will go back on your normal schedule."

"You could have told me." I got out of the car and slammed the door.

"Baby, I am sorry."

I ignored her and walked inside. I sat in a chair while she checked me in; then she came and sat next to me.

"Are you going to be mad at me all day?"

I picked up a magazine and started flipping through it. When I was called in, I did not look at her; she followed right behind me.

"These are a copy of her records from New York City."

"Thank you, Mrs. Delecroie. Has everything been going okay?"

"Yes, she has been fine. Full of energy."

"Good, we are just going to do a quick checkup."

He determined everything was fine. I walked out of the office and straight to the car without saying a word.

"Tanya, I am sorry. I know you hate doctors; I am just trying to make it easier."

"Well, don't." When we got home, I went straight to my room and shut the door. Hope knocked on our connection door. "I don't want to talk to anyone."

At 6 p.m., Mom came into my room. I ignored her and continued to read my book.

"Everyone is in the dining room, waiting for you."

"Not hungry."

"How long are you going to be angry?"

"Don't know."

"Fine, when you have decided you have been angry long enough, you know where to find us. Until then, you can stay in your room." She left, shutting the door. She returned just before 9 p.m. carrying a plate of fruit.

"I thought you might be hungry."

"Nope."

"Tanya, I know you are not happy about the doctor, but you are overreacting."

"Wonder where I get that from?"

"All right, we are not leaving until we settle this, young lady."

"Fine."

"What is really bothering you?"

"Like you don't know."

"Baby, I really don't."

"You say you trust me, you are not going to keep secrets from me. Then surprise, we are at the doctor's."

"You are right, I should have told you. I just did not want to upset you. I was not thinking. I will not do it again."

"Don't do it again."

"All right, I promise. Now drink this milk."

I took it from her and drank it, then ate some fruit. Hope and Sara were walking by the room; I called them in. We all sat on my bed.

"Mom, would you read us a book?"

"I would love to."

Sara and I started taking morning rides together. Instead of giving us a tutor for the summer, Mom gave us a list of things she wanted us to complete and said that she would be checking to make sure we were following through. If we did not, then she would hire a tutor. Three weeks after we returned, Elizabeth went off to a college prep summer camp. Craig returned to New York for some business. We were starting to get restless. We were never allowed off the property.

"Mom, please can we go to town, go shopping? We are bored."

"How can you be bored? You have everything you can want here."

"No stores."

"Girls, I have to work. I cannot take you today."

"Mom, we are going into eighth grade, and we have gone to boarding school; I think we will be able to go shopping by ourselves."

"Girls."

"Mom, we will all stay together, and we all have our cell phones."

"Fine, straight there, three hours, then back home. I will have the town car pick you up in twenty minutes out front."

"Thank you!" We all gave her a hug, then ran out of the room.

"I love you all!" she yelled behind us. We got our things, then ran down to the car. David, the part-time driver, was waiting.

Chapter Twelve

"Tanya, open your eyes, baby, come on."

I did as I was asked. Mom was standing over me.

"What happened? Where am I?"

"You are in the hospital; you were in an accident."

"Hope and Sara?"

"Baby, you are going to be fine; the doctor is just going to check you over."

"But, Mom."

The doctor stepped up and started going over my reflexes. When I looked again, Ann was standing where Mom had been.

"You are going to be fine. Miss Delecroie, I am going to release your sister. I want her to go home and to bed; she needs some rest. I will give her some medication to calm her for now." Ann nodded.

"Thank you. I will tell my mother, then I will take her home."

He nodded and walked out.

"What happened?"

"A drunk driver ran a red light, hit your car."

"How are Hope and Sara?"

"I am not sure, stay here. I will be right back; then I am taking you home." She turned and left.

I got out of bed and followed her. I was a little lightheaded, but I wanted to see what was going on. Ann stopped next to Mom. She was talking to another doctor. I was behind them so they did not see me. I could tell Mom was crying. She and Ann were holding each other.

"They are releasing Tanya."

"At least I have her; it is amazing that she is all right."

"How is Hope?"

"She is still in surgery. They said they would let me know as soon as they knew anything. Is your father on his way?"

"Yes, he was going to pick up Kate and Elizabeth and bring them home."

"If only I had said no. I should not have let them go."

"Mom, you had no idea, there was no way to predict this."

"Sara is gone, Hope is fighting for her life, and I should have said no!"

It took a moment for me to comprehend what they said. Sara was gone—gone where? Then I realized. "WHERE IS SARA?"

They both turned to look at me; I fell to my knees, crying; it all seemed to be slow motion. Mom came over and wrapped her arms around me; I cried. Then I felt a poke in my arm; I turned my head to see the doctor with a needle.

"I am so sorry, baby." Mom held me.

I woke up in my bed. The room was dark. Ann was sitting on the couch reading a book; she put it down when I sat up.

"You are awake."

"Yes, please tell me it was all a lie."

"I am sorry," she said, coming over to me.

"What about Hope?"

"She is out of surgery. She is going to pull through. Now why don't you go back to sleep?" She handed me a glass of water and a pill.

When I woke up again, the sun was shining through the window. Mom was sitting next to me. "How are you doing?"

"Okay."

"What time is it?"

"Ten a.m."

"Hope and Sa…"

"Hope is fine; she slept through the night, and I am going to take you up to see her. Elizabeth and your dad are there now. Ann is in bed; she stayed up with you all night."

"Oh."

"Go get dressed and we will go."

Kate went with us; Lizzy met us in the hall outside of Hope's room. She gave me a hug. Dad came out and gave me a hug as well. "Tanya, I am so glad that you are okay."

"Craig, how is Hope doing?"

"She is sleeping now; she is doing well."

"Good. I am going to take Tanya in." She put her arm around me and opened the door. Seeing Hope in the bed, hooked up to all of the machines, it hit me hard. Reality hit me at that moment. Sara would not be coming back. She was gone. Hope was hurt badly. I started to cry.

"Baby, it is going to be okay."

"Sara," I mumbled.

She pulled me into a closer hug. "I know. I miss her. We all will." I looked up at her; she was crying as well.

Hope slept the entire time I was there. Kate took me home after about an hour. Mom said that she had some arrangements to make, then she would be home. When I got home, I sat on my couch and stared out of the window. I was in a daze.

"She has not moved since we got home."

"That was seven hours ago."

"I know."

Mom sat down next to me. "Baby, we need to talk." I did not move. "First about Hope: The doctor said that she is paralyzed." I looked at her. "She will not be able to walk, but they said it was just temporary." She took my hand and kissed it.

"I also need to talk to you about Sara." She had tears coming down her cheeks.

I shook my head no.

"Yes, we have to. I had to make the arrangements for her funeral. It is going to be the day after tomorrow. Hope will still be in the hospital, so she will not be able to go."

I shook my head no again and started crying.

"I think you should go." I cried harder; she rocked me and held onto me.

I woke up in my bed. Mom was sleeping next to me, her arms still wrapped around me.

"Hi, baby. I did not want you out of my sight." She walked to my closet. "Why don't you get dressed, and then I will take you to see Hope."

When we arrived at the hospital, Dad was leaving. "Hello, Kerstin, Tanya." He gave Mom a hug.

"How is Hope?"

"She is doing better. She is awake, and she wants some real food for breakfast, so I am going to get her some takeout."

"That is good." I sat down in a nearby chair. "How is she dealing with all of this?"

"I do not think she realizes it yet; she has been though a lot."

"What about her legs?"

"She does understand that; the physical therapist talked to her about it last night."

"All right, they are putting a lift in the house this morning and a ramp out front. I also made arrangements for the classroom to be turned into a place for her physical therapy."

"Good. How is Tanya doing?"

"She had not said anything since yesterday; I am worried about her."

"We will keep an eye on her."

They were both looking at me, then Mom extended a hand to me. "Tanya, come, baby, we are going up now." I walked into Hope's room and gave her a hug.

She smiled at me. "The doctor said that I could go home soon if I keep up this recovery."

"I know, darling, but that does not mean you are healed. You still have a long way to go. I am hiring a nurse, and you will have physical therapy."

"I know, but I can go home and be with my sisters."

"Hope, sweetie, do you remember what we talked about?" She looked at me; I knew what she was thinking. She sensed what I felt, and she started crying.

"I know, Mommy. I just don't want to…"

Mom sat on the bed and held Hope the same way she had held me.

At home I noticed the ramp, then on the stairs was the chair lift.

"Hi, Mom, Tanya." Kate appeared from the den.

"Hello, Kate, is everything finished?"

"Yes, they just finished. The nurse also dropped off some things."

"Good. I want this to be a smooth transition for Hope."

I started walking up the stairs.

"Tanya, you need to eat lunch; come with me into the dining room."

I shook my head no and continued up the stairs.

"Mom, she will be okay; missing one meal is not going to hurt her."

"She was not physically hurt, but I am not sure that mentally she can handle another blow; this one has almost destroyed her."

"She is strong, and we are all here for her; she will be okay. How is Hope?"

"All right. I really do not think that she has really grasped Sara."

I quit listening and went to my room. I lay on my bed and focused on my safe place. No one could hurt me. I was untouchable.

"Tanya, Tanya, look at me."

I blinked and turned my head to see Mom sitting there.

"Where were you, baby?" I shrugged my shoulders. "Dinner is ready; let's go down." I shook my head no. "You skipped lunch, so you have to eat dinner." I shook my head no again. "Fine." She went to my phone and ordered a meal to be brought up, then she started going through my closet. Within five minutes, the food was dropped off.

"Tanya, I am not leaving until you eat your dinner." She could tell I wanted to be alone and was using it against me. I picked up a fork and ate the food. "Thank you, now I will go. I know you want to be alone. So I will let you be. It is getting late; why don't you get ready for bed? Goodnight, baby."

Mom woke me up in the morning; she was wearing a black dress suit, her hair tied back. "Baby, you have to get up, we have to leave in an hour."

I nodded my head and sat up.

"Breakfast is on the table. Have a seat and I will do your hair."

When she was done, I changed into a black dress, and then we walked to the den. Dad and William were also wearing black suits; Elizabeth, Ann, and Kate were all wearing black dresses. We arrived at the church in the limo. Mom took my hand as we walked to the front of the already crowded church. Sara's casket was covered in flowers; there was a large picture of her. After the service and the cemetery, everyone was invited back to our house. I sat on the couch. My tears were gone; I had already cried them away that day. I was surprised how many girls from school came. Several people that I knew and did not know all came over to tell me how sorry they were.

Mom walked in with the priest, they both looked over at me, and then he came over to see me. "Tanya, please know that your sister will always be with you. You just need to keep her in your heart." I shook my head. "If you ever want to talk, please give me a call, or come and see me." I just looked at him.

I set myself on autopilot. I did what I was told, ate when I was told to, but mostly I sat on the couch in my room and stared into space. Mom would come tell me when I was to go to the dining room, or when it was time for bed and time to get up. I did not read or watch television, I did nothing.

Three days after the funeral, they brought Hope home. After she was settled, I went to see her. I was there for a moment when her nurse, Mrs. Morris, told me she needed her rest and kicked me out. I was walking down to the den when I heard my name coming from Mom's room. I walked over and listened through the door. She was talking to Dad.

"I am not sure what to do with her; she is not just devastated or depressed, she seems to be out of emotions. She has withdrawn. I am not sure if any of us can get through to her. She is no longer smiling, laughing, or even crying."

"I know. She seems to be just going through the motions."

"So what do we do?"

"I think we should give her just a little bit more time to snap out of it, then we look into a doctor."

"She hates doctors."

"I know, but if we cannot help her, we have to find someone who can."

"I need to go check on her."

I hurried back to my room. I stayed in my safe place for the next five days. I tried to see Hope, but Mrs. Morris always had an excuse for me to stay away. That day, I returned to my room after lunch, and Mom followed me. She took my hand and we sat on the couch.

"Tanya, your father and I are worried about you. Hope says that you have not even come over to see her. We want to have you speak to someone." I shook my head no. "Baby, I do not know what else to do."

I looked at her, then took her hand and headed towards Hope's room. Before I opened the door, I let go of her hand and gave her the motion to stay where she was. I opened the door; Mrs. Morris was standing there.

"Tanya, I thought I told you to stay away? Your sister needs her rest."

"Mrs. Morris, pack your things and be out in an hour."

"Mrs. Delecroie, I was not aware that you were there."

"Obviously, I hired you to assist in the wellbeing of my children, both mental and physical. By keeping Hope and Tanya apart, it is not only hurting Hope's mental state, but also Tanya's, so get your things and get out. You are fired." Mrs. Morris turned and left. "I am sorry about that, baby. I have to go hire another nurse. Hope is still asleep, but you can stay if you want." She kissed my forehead and left. I crawled into bed with Hope; she was the only person who knew how I was feeling.

Chapter Thirteen

I must have fallen asleep because when I woke up, I heard Mom and Dad's voices. I kept my eyes closed.

"They look like angles."

"I know. I was getting use to having all of them here again; now Sara is gone, and we are back to two. I cannot believe that lady treated Tanya like she did. Did she think Tanya had not been through enough?"

"I do not know."

"Mom, Dad, Nurse Peck is here."

"Thank you, Kate. Miss Peck, thank you for coming so quickly."

"No problem, and please call me Emily."

"Emily, they are sleeping, Hope is on the right—she is the one we spoke about—and Tanya is on the left. She has not spoken since the accident."

"I am sure Tanya is feeling helpless for her sister."

"Hope is the oldest; she has always been protective of the other two. Tanya is the youngest; she is also in remission from leukemia. Your main responsibility is Hope; however, I do expect that you keep both of their interests in mind."

"Absolutely. They have been through enough, no need for any more traumas."

"Good. This door goes into the room set up for Hope's physical therapy; the other side leads into Tanya's room. Are you ready to meet them?"

"Oh, yes."

"All right."

I opened my eyes when Mom stated stroking my hair. "Hi, baby." She kissed my forehead, then leaned over to wake up Hope. "Girls, this is Emily Peck, the new nurse."

"Hi, girls, you can call me Emily."

"Hello," Hope answered; I just nodded my head. She smiled at us, then Mom opened her mouth.

"Tanya, will you please come downstairs with me and eat dinner?" I looked at Hope, who then nodded.

"Mom, she wants to eat with me."

Mom pushed the hair behind my ears. "I will send it up, if you promise to eat."

"Mrs. Delecroie, I think both girls should eat downstairs, with the family."

"I would love that; however, we were told that it was too soon for Hope to go downstairs."

"The only way for her to recover is for her to get back to a normal life."

I sat up on the bed and watched as Emily helped Hope into the wheelchair; then she showed Hope how to use the chair lift. Mom invited Emily to join us for dinner; however, Emily declined, saying she was going to go unpack.

"Tanya, how do you like Emily?"

"Tanya likes her much better than mean old Mrs. Morris."

"If I ask Hope a question, will you answer? I miss the sound of your voice."

"Craig, please give her some time."

"Tanya, I am sorry."

After dinner, Hope was tired so Emily took her up to get ready for bed. I went back to my room and picked out a book.

"Well, this is an improvement; lately you have done nothing but stare into space. So I will take you reading a book." I closed the book and looked at her. "I talked to Keri's mom; she said to let you know they are all thinking about you. I told them we would reschedule Keri's trip soon."

I nodded my head.

"Mrs. Delecroie, Hope is in bed for the night. Is there anything Tanya needs?"

"No, thank you. I will get her into bed." Emily left. "I think you should be getting ready for bed also, so why don't you go change, and I will order some ice cream! As a treat." I smiled at her, and she smiled back.

In the morning, there was no outfit sitting out for me, so I chose one, then went into Hope's room. Emily was already in there.

"Good morning, Tanya. Would you do me a favor and get Hope out an outfit to wear?" I did as she asked; she helped Hope get dressed. Then she made us all go down to the dining room for breakfast. Every morning after breakfast, Emily would work with Hope, and I would read a book. When Hope would take a nap in the afternoon, Emily would play board games with me. On a rare occasion, I would go horseback riding with Elizabeth. Hope became more and more independent; Emily even had her trying to walk with the bars. Every night, Mom came and sat with me. One night in mid August, she came in and sat with me.

"Tanya, I am not sure what to do. You are supposed to start at school next week. Hope is going to be home schooled; what am I going to do with you? It has been two months since you last spoke. I cannot send you to school; do you want to stay home with a tutor?"

I looked at her; I could read on her face that she really was in a dilemma. I had never seen that look on her face. She was always in control and always knew what she wanted or what she was going to do.

"Should I keep you here? Or should I enroll you at St. Margaret's?" I knew she was rephrasing it as a question to herself, not to me. She did not expect me to answer her.

"I want to go to school, but I want to be with Hope."

She threw her arms around me. "Oh, Tanya! I have been waiting so long to hear your voice again."

"I know."

"Why don't we keep you home? It will give you more time, and you will be closer to Hope. If she is ready, then maybe in January we can get you back into the Premier or at least St. Margaret's." I nodded my head in agreement. She hugged me again. "I love you, baby."

I did start speaking on occasion, but only to Mom or Hope.

The following week, I started my lessons with a tutor. Hope and I each had our own instructors. Mom had told mine not to expect me to speak to him, but I decided it was time to start to open up again. I would finish my lessons around 4 p.m, then I would go see Hope. Dad was excited the first time I said anything to him; he gave me a hug. On Friday, I was heading up to see Hope when Mom stopped me.

"Baby, how were your lessons?"

"All right."

"Are you learning anything?"

"Yes."

"Good."

"I am going to see Hope."

"She is asleep. You have a checkup, so why don't you play with her when we get home?"

"She is awake; I can at least say hi."

"I was just up there; she is sleeping."

"She is awake."

"All right, let's go check." We walked up to her room; she was sitting on the couch, watching TV.

"Hi, Tanya! Mom."

"Hope, did you rest long enough?"

"Yes, Mom, I am not sick."

"All right, honey. I am taking Tanya in for a checkup, your father will be back in about an hour, and Elizabeth and Ann are both here if you need anything. Emily will not be back until after dinner."

"I know. I will be fine" Mom gave her a kiss, then we left. The doctor's appointment went normally.

"Mom?"

"Yes, baby?"

"When can we reschedule Keri's visit?"

"Are you up to it?"

"Yes."

"All right, I will call her mother and see if she can take a long weekend and come down on Friday."

"Thank you!" We pulled through the gates. I ran inside as Elizabeth was coming down the stairs.

"Hey, Hope said to tell you that she is down by the pool."

Mom was behind me. "At the pool by herself? Elizabeth, what were you thinking?"

"Dad is with her."

"Oh, I am sorry, darling. Why don't we all go down there and have a pool party?"

"Okay."

"You girls go ahead. I have a phone call to make, and then I will be in."

When Elizabeth and I walked in, Hope was floating on a noodle chair. Dad was splashing her. She was laughing.

"Tanya, Lizzy, he is getting me wet!" Lizzy and I looked at each other, then we ran and jumped into the pool. I splashed both of them!

"Now you are going to get it!" Dad grabbed me and swung me around in the water. I started laughing while trying to get away. He tossed me a little ways. "I have missed that laugh!"

In all of my time here I had not seen this side of him. I liked it.

Mom walked in with Kate and Ann. "Now is this is a sight? I ordered pizza for dinner, girls."

"Kerstin, what are we celebrating?"

"Tanya is still in remission, and Kate is leaving tomorrow, back to New York."

"What, is my son-in-law upset about not seeing his wife?"

"NO, Dad, I miss him. It is time to get back."

"Oh, well, all right. Now," he said, grabbing me again, "you are a reason to celebrate!" He swung me around again in the water. I had more fun than I had had in a long time. When I got to my room, I was exhausted; I was climbing into bed when Mom came in.

"I thought I should let you know. Keri's mom said that it would be fine for her to come this weekend."

"Thank you."

"You're welcome; now you are off to bed, baby."

"Mom, I am almost 14."

"Yes, you are."

"Are you going to stop calling me baby?"

"Probably not."

"Oh."

"Goodnight." She kissed my forehead, then left.

It rained all weekend, so we had to stay inside. We played games, and I read some of my books. Classes were the same all week. Hope and I did our homework together, then we would play games.

At noon on Friday, there was a knock on the library door. Mom opened the door; standing next to her was Keri.

"Keri!" I got up and ran over to her.

Mom looked at my instructor. "Mr. Mede could you…"

"No problem. Class is over."

"Tanya, I have to go do a bit of work. You two have fun."

"Thanks, Mom." She left. Keri and I started walking.

"I cannot believe that you live here; this place is huge."

"I know. We will go back to my room first, then you have to meet Hope."

"What were you doing in there?"

"School."

"I thought you were going to some private school?"

"Mom and I decided I was not ready to start at Premier. She decided to have me home schooled for a semester."

"Wow, do you get lost here?"

"No, it is pretty easy. Here is my room." I opened the double doors, and she walked in.

"This room is bigger than my house!"

"It is big; it has a walk-in closet and also a full bath."

"Wow."

"How did you get here?"

"Your mom picked me up and flew with me here on a private jet!"

"Kind of cool, huh?"

"Kind of? Totally! Your mom is really nice."

"I know. You want to go swimming?"

"It is cold outside."

"Who said anything about outside?"

"You have an indoor pool? I did not bring a suit."

"That is okay, you can have one of mine. I will never wear them all anyways." She was walking around my room. "I cannot believe that while we were growing up, there were two girls that looked exactly like you living not all that far away."

"I know."

She picked up a picture of all of us. "How do you tell them apart?"

"I just know, always have. When I first saw them again I knew immediately, but Dad has a cheaters way to tell us apart." I picked up another picture of us and showed it to her. "What do you see?"

"You are all there, dressed alike except for the color."

"Yup, he color coordinates us so he can tell quickly who is who." She started laughing. We went swimming for the afternoon.

When we arrived back at my room, Mom was at the door. "I was just looking for you. Are you having fun?"

"Yes."

"Thank you, Mrs. Delecroie, for letting me come."

"Keri, it is my pleasure. Tanya, your father just called. He is bringing an associate home for dinner. Could you please lend Keri one of your dinner dresses?"

"Can't we just eat up here?"

"Sorry, baby, they are bringing their daughter."

"All right."

"Hope is just finishing up with her studies, and Elizabeth should be home shortly."

"Thanks, Mom. I am going to introduce Keri and Hope."

"Run along. Just make sure you get ready in one hour."

"We will."

Keri and I walked over to Hope's room; the door was open so we walked in. "Hi, guys. You must be Keri."

"Yes, I am, and you are Hope."

"It is nice to meet you. Tanya talks about you all of the time."

We hung out in Hope's room for a while and talked. Elizabeth joined us when she got home. Then we started playing cards.

"Why are you not getting ready?"

We all looked up to see Ann in the door.

"What time is it?"

"Five-thirty, Liz. Now go before Mom comes this way. Tanya, and you must be Keri, hurry. Mom will be up to do your hair in less than fifteen minutes. Where is Emily?"

"Keri, this is my sister Ann, and Ann, it is Friday. Emily gets the weekends off now; she is out visiting someone."

Keri and I went back to my room and changed. Mom was coming in just as we finished.

"Cutting it kind of close, baby?"

"Sorry, Mom."

"It is all right. You remember Mackenzie Prince?"

"You mean the girl who has nothing but questions about things that are none of her business?"

"Yes, well, she will be here in ten minutes."

"You didn't tell me it was her."

"Did not, and no, I did not."

"I am starting to feel ill."

"Oh, no, I am going to have to send Keri home."

"Mom, she is really annoying."

"Be nice, put up with her, and I will take you both shopping tomorrow."

"Fine."

"Thank you, baby. Now, are you both ready?"

"Yes."

"Good, head downstairs. I am going to go check on Hope, and then I will be down."

When we got to the bottom of the stairs, the door opened, and Dad appeared with his guest.

"Hello, Tanya."

"Hello, Father."

"You remember Mr. and Mrs. Prince, their daughter, Mackenzie?"

"Yes, it is very nice to see you all again. This is my friend Keri; she is staying with us this weekend."

We made it through dinner without any incidents, and then Mom had us go to the recreation room. Ann stayed with the adults. Elizabeth asked to, but was told no.

"I have to have surgery on my hand. I have to stay in the hospital overnight, can you believe that? Of course, Mom says that it is really nothing. My dad said that your parents should have signed you up for hospital points like at a hotel. They said that you are always in and out of the hospital, and now with your sister. Mom said that your parents cannot catch a break."

"Tanya, what is she talking about?" Keri asked.

"You know, because of her leukemia."

Elizabeth jumped up. "Mackenzie, I do not think you should be speaking to Tanya of such things; it is not very nice."

"Well, my parents talk about how your parents are cursed."

"Mackenzie Prince, you apologize to Tanya, then to Mr. and Mrs. Delecroie. Then wait for us in the car."

She did as she was told. Mr. and Mrs. Prince apologized and left.

"All right, girls, it is getting late. Time for bed. Keri, I have set up a guestroom for you; why don't I show you where it is?"

I changed into my pajamas when Mom came in. "Are you ready for bed?"

"Yes."

"What is wrong?"

"Keri did not know about my being sick; then Mackenzie said I had Leukemia. I know she is going to have questions."

"Then why don't we go talk about it? Mackenzie has always had a big mouth. I am sorry."

We went and talked to Keri. She was upset that she had not known, but when I explained my reasons, she was okay with it. She agreed not to tell the Johnsons, to let me when I was ready. She was just pretty relieved that I was okay now.

Saturday, Mom did take us shopping, She bought us both some books and games. Keri was overwhelmed, but Mom assured her that she did not mind. That afternoon we all watched a movie in the theater. Sunday we had brunch, then Keri had to go. I spent the afternoon working on my homework. Monday went back to normal. Hope was making some great improvements! She was starting to feel her legs more and was taking a few steps on her own with no help.

Chapter Fourteen

Two weeks went by very fast, then it was September 5th. Mom woke me up. "Happy birthday, baby!"

"Morning, Mom."

"Baby, normally I make you wait until after dinner, but would you like to sneak a present now?"

"YES!"

She handed me a box. I opened it. Inside was a locket. I opened the locket. The one side had a picture of Hope, Sara, and I; the other was a picture of just Sara. I gave mom a hug and started crying.

"Thank you. I miss her so much."

"I know, baby, I miss her too. I am just thankful that I did not lose all of you. Today is your birthday. No more sad thoughts." I attended my normal studies, then Hope and I played games. We decided to go out front for a while and wait for Elizabeth to come home. After a half hour, a car pulled up out front. It was not Elizabeth's.

"I hope Dad did not invite his associates to dinner tonight."

"Me too."

The car came to a stop, then I realized who it was. "Hope, go get Mom."

"What is wrong?"

"Just go get Mom. Hurry."

She disappeared into the house. The car door opened; Liz and Jeff Johnson got out. Sam and Isabelle were in the back seat. I stood up and looked at them, then Mom came running outside.

"Baby, what is wrong?" She paused when she saw them. "Mr. and Mrs. Johnson, what can we do for you?"

Jeff started up the stairs; Mom wrapped her arms around me. "We are here for Tanya, our daughter."

"I am sorry, I do not understand."

"We have a court order for temporary visitation. We are suing for custody."

"What?"

"Tanya, calm down. Mr. Johnson, this is ridiculous; a court order was not necessary. If you wanted to see her, all you had to do was call. Why would you want to add more chaos to her life?"

"Her life has been nothing but chaos since she moved in with you. We want to give her a normal life again."

"Tanya, I want you to go inside."

"She is coming with us."

"You want to see her, fine, but not tonight. She has plans."

"That can wait. She is coming with us."

"I am not a piece of property." I broke free from Mom's hold and ran inside.

"If you really cared about that little girl, you would realize that today is her birthday. She is spending it with her sister and this family. As for your court order, you may contact my lawyer. Now if you will excuse me, I have to go comfort my daughter."

I sat on the couch in the den.

"Baby, I said no more sad thoughts today."

"Why are they doing this now?"

"I do not know, but do not worry about it; we will take care of it."

"They do not know who I am now, and I."

She wrapped her arms around me. "Hush, I told you not to worry. Are you ready for dinner? And then presents?"

"I guess."

"You guess? Is that how excited you are?" She started tickling me. I started laughing.

"Yes! Yes, I am!"

"That is better. Let's go find your sisters so we can get started."

Hope and I both received lots of gifts! The best one of all was Hope walking around the room. I was exhausted and fell asleep as soon as my head hit the pillow.

I slept in in the morning. I was walking toward the den when I heard voices from Dad's office. I peaked my head in, but they did not notice me.

"They are claiming neglect and an unstable home."

"That is insane!"

"They really do not have a claim."

"How can they? She is our little girl."

"They think they do have a right, and they are claiming that the biological connection should not matter since they adopted her, and she is theirs."

"She was kidnapped."

"They have a good lawyer."

"I am not losing her; that is not a choice."

"Kerstin, do not worry. I will keep it tied up in court until she is 18 if I have to. They are not taking our little girl away." He turned and saw me standing in the door. "Tanya, we did not see you."

"I know."

"Why don't you come in? We need to see how you feel."

I walked into the room, and Mom met me and put her arm around me. "Baby, what do you want? This is your life."

"I love them, and I miss them. However, they do not know me; they are the ones who have neglected me the past six months. I want to stay; this is where I belong. With my family. I will tell the judge if I have to."

The phone rang before anyone responded. Dad answered it. "NOT a chance!...We want it supervised...I do not care; they have not spoken to her in six months...NO, they always have had access to her; it is their own faults...Fine, two hours at the hotel pool." Dad hung up the phone and turned to me. "They want to see you today at their hotel."

"All right."

Two hours later, I was in the hotel.

"Baby, we will be in the dining room if you need anything."

"Okay." I walked from them across the lobby to where the Johnsons were standing. They embraced me, but all of the sudden our roles were reversed. I did not embrace them back. It was like the first time Mom had given me a hug.

"Tanya, we have missed you so much."

"You have ignored my emails and do not answer my phone calls."

"I am sorry, we did not want you to worry about what we were planning. I mean, you do have to live with these people."

"These people are my parents, and I love them." Keri had kept her word and not told them about my illness.

"So, Tanya, why are you not going to school?"

"I am in school; it is just in my home."

"You need a school with other children, not a home. That is just one more reason we need to get you back to a normal home."

"My home is normal, and I like being there with my sisters."

"You have two more sisters."

"Sam ignores me, and as for Isabelle, you got her after I left."

"Well, you will know her better after you move back in with us."

"You do not listen, do you?"

"Those people have brainwashed you against us."

"For the last time, those people are MY PARENTS! And they have never said a bad thing about you."

"You will understand when you are back in a stable life."

I had had enough; I got up from my chair and ran out of the pool area, through the lobby, and to the dining room. Mom saw me coming. By the time I reached her table, she took me into her arms.

"What is wrong? Baby, calm down."

"Can we just go home?"

"Of course, we will take you home. I will just pay the bill." Mom took me to the ladies room to clean up. When we returned, Jeff and Dad were standing face to face in the lobby. Liz was behind them with Isabelle.

"Our visitation says we get her for the whole afternoon; we still have a few hours left."

"My daughter has expressed that she is upset, and I am taking her home."

"She is a child; you spoil children when they get everything they want."

"Tanya is a young lady, and it has never hurt to spoil them once in a while. We are taking her home, and if you have anything else to say, you can contact my lawyer. Kerstin, Tanya, let's go." I did not say anything, just followed him out.

At home, I went to the library and picked up a book.

"Tanya, do you want to talk about it?"

"No."

"I do not want you to worry about this; I want you to go back to being the happy young lady you were a year ago."

"A lot has happened in a year."

"Yes, it has." She kissed the top of my head. "I love you," she said and walked out.

Emily joined our family for brunch on Sunday; Kate was there also. I am sure Dad called her home for her legal spin on things. Emily decided that this was the day for Hope to quit relying on her chair and start walking more. That made Mom quite happy. Over the next two weeks, I did not hear anything concerning the Johnsons. Hope was going to bed early because she was tired from walking so much. I continued my normal studies and also spent some time practicing the piano. That Friday, Mom came into the library.

"Mr. Mede, how are her studies going?"

"Very well, Mrs. Delecroie."

"Can you please put together a progress report and an outline of what you are covering?"

"Yes, ma'am."

"Tanya, let's take a walk. We need to talk." I followed her to Dad's office; he was sitting at his desk. Kate was sitting in a chair. "Tanya, have a seat."

"What is going on?"

"We thought you should know what is going on."

"Oh."

"We have a hearing on Monday concerning a temporary custody arrangement."

"I do not want to go back."

"We know. I think you and your sisters should be there."

"All right."

"Do you have any questions?"

"May I go to my room?"

"All right, baby."

I ran all the way to Hope's room and told her what was going on. Emily decided that it would be good for us both to go horseback riding, so that is what we did. We returned to the house just before dinner. Over the weekend, nothing was mentioned about Monday. The only think anybody talked about was how we were going to spend Thanksgiving vacation. Hope, Elizabeth, and I voted on a cruise. Everyone agreed.

Chapter Fifteen

We arrived at the courthouse Monday morning at 8:30 a.m. Hope and I were wearing white blouses, navy skirts, knee-high socks, and headbands. Elizabeth was dressed similarly, Craig was wearing a suit, and Mom was wearing a navy dress suit. Three men met us outside of the courtroom. The Johnsons were already seated. Isabelle and Sam were not present. We went to the other side of the room and sat down. They were staring at Hope and me. Everyone stood when the Judge entered.

"Ladies and gentleman, we are here to decide the custody of Tanya Alexandra Delecroie."

"Your Honor, two years ago my clients were informed that their young daughter's adoption was not legal, and her biological parents wanted the child back. Reluctantly, they agreed. They did not want Tanya to be put through a custody battle. However, they have come to believe their daughter has been neglected and that her life has been unstable since going to live with the Delecroies."

"Craig and Kerstin love all of their children and would do anything for them. They did not ask for their baby girl to be kidnapped and placed up for adoption. Naturally, when they found her, they wanted her back. She is their daughter and their youngest child."

"Mr. and Mrs. Johnson, you say that she is neglected. How?"

"Your Honor, they sent her away to boarding school. She is never in one place long enough to get used to her surroundings."

"Your Honor, Tanya asked to go to boarding school, and yes, the Delecroie's have three houses, in which Tanya has her own room in all. These girls are learning diversity."

"Is Tanya present?"

Mom motioned for me to stand up; I did and replied, "Yes, sir."

"Please come up here." I walked up to the stand. "Tanya, I would like to speak with you in my chambers, is that all right?"

"Yes, sir." He got up and I followed him. His chambers looked a lot like Craig's office. "Please have a seat." I did. "Tanya, I want to know what you think. How do you feel?"

"Sir, when I was first told that I had been kidnapped and the judge said I was to be returned to the Delecroies, I was terrified. I did not know them, I did not want to go, and the Johnsons were my family. When I first moved in with them, I was scared, but I knew they loved me. I would have had to be blind and deaf not to realize that. I knew my sisters without question. Hope, Sara, and I belonged with each other. I was never told that I could not talk to the Johnsons. As a matter of fact, last spring my mom arranged for me to spend my spring break with them. That was when they started treating me weirdly. They were always short when they talked to me and they were always saying bad things about my parents. That is when I decided that I would limit my contact with them. I was tired of feeling in the center; I love my sisters and my parents. Both sets. I have missed so much time with my real family. I want to be with them."

"Your parents recently took you away from a court-ordered visitation with the Johnsons."

"I asked them to take me home. The Johnsons were saying mean things about my parents and said that I had been brainwashed. I ran out to my Mom, crying. I could not take it anymore."

We went back into the courtroom, and I took my seat between my mom and Hope.

"I have read the statements from both parties, and by talking to Tanya, my speculation was confirmed. Tanya Alexandra Delecroie will remain in the custody of her biological parents, Kerstin and Craigory Delecroie. There is no sign of neglect; this court cannot justify removing the child from her current situation." I hugged Hope and then Mom and Dad. I looked over and saw Liz and Jeff hugging each other.

"I will be right back." Mom squeezed my hand and smiled at me. I walked over to them. "Just because I want to be with them does not mean that I do not love you anymore. You were my parents for ten years, and that means everything to me; however, I have missed so much time with them, they love me, and I love them. I miss spending time with you; however, every time I do, all you do is say bad things about them. I tried to tell you this at the hotel, but you would not listen; maybe you will now." I turned and rejoined my family. We went out to lunch to celebrate.

Over the next few weeks, I kept very busy. Hope no longer had physical therapy as part of her daily lessons, so we finished our studies about the same time. We played games and went horseback riding and swimming every day. I was keeping myself so busy that I was exhausted by the time I went to bed. In the beginning of November, I woke up in the middle of the night, sweating and burning up. I got out of bed and walked down to Mom's room.

"Mom," I said, standing in the door.

"What is wrong, Tanya?"

"I do not feel very well."

She got out of bed and walked over to me and she placed her hand on my head. "My god, Craig, she is burning up." She sat me down on their bed while they both went and changed, then Craig picked me up.

"I will meet you in the car. I am going to tell Ann that we are taking her to the ER."

I was asleep before we got into the car. I woke up in the hospital bed. "Tanya, we are going to put an IV in your arm." I shook my head, but was ignored.

"Doctor, she is in remission from leukemia."

"Okay, I need to do some tests. Tanya, I am going to draw some blood."

I shook my head again. When he was done, I fell asleep again with Mom stroking my hair. The doctor woke me up when he reentered the room.

"Mr. And Mrs. Delecroie, I am sorry to tell you Tanya is no longer in remission; the leukemia is back."

I started crying.

"Baby, everything will be all right."

"We are going to admit her to bring down her fever, and then we will refer you back to the doctor on her case."

"Thank you, doctor." He left, and Mom sat down on the bed and took me into her arms.

"Can we still go on the cruise?"

Craig started laughing. "We will have to see, but we will take you on a cruise."

"Good."

"Baby, close your eyes and go to sleep. When this fever is gone, we can take you home."

When I woke up again, I could see Mom outside of the door, talking to some one. "You are awake," she said, entering the room. "How do you feel?" Beside her was my doctor from New York.

"Better."

"Good." She walked over to the bed and picked up my hand. "Baby, your doctor and I have been talking, and we have decided that you are going to go through chemo again."

"No, MOM, that made me so sick, and I do not want to be in the hospital."

She squeezed my hand and smiled at me. "I know, but we need to do what is best for you. There is another hospital here that is all about child leukemia. We are going to have you go there, and you will only be in the hospital for a little time, Emily has agreed to stay on and help with you, and if we start in two days, the first round will be done so we can go on that cruise."

"Mrs. Delecroie, you know I advise against that."

"Yes, but Tanya has had her heart set on it."

"Mom, I do not want chemo."

"I know." She bent down and kissed my forehead, then the nurse walked in.

"Mrs. Delecroie, your husband has just finished the paperwork; she is free to go. Just remember, lots of rest."

Hope was waiting for us when we entered the house. "Ann said they took you to the hospital. It is back, isn't it?" I looked up at her; she knew without my responding. She gave me a hug.

"Girls, Tanya needs to go up to bed and rest."

Hope and I both went to my room, and she got out a deck of cards. "So we will play in your room now." She smiled and climbed onto my bed. "Tanya, what is going to happen?"

"I do not know. They said that we could still go on the cruise. However, Mom said I have to go back through chemo."

"Another hospital."

"Yes."

"Well, we will have to focus on the cruise."

Emily knocked on the door and then came in. "I guess you girls want to make sure I stay in work." We both started laughing. "Hope, you have some studies to go do, and Tanya, you need to rest." She opened up her hand and gave me some pills, then gave me a glass of water. I took them, looked at Hope, and she smiled, then she left. I slept for a bit and then watched some TV. Late in the afternoon, Mom finally came up to see me.

"How are you doing, baby?"

"Fine. Is supper ready?"

"It will be soon; do you want something sent up?"

"I may be sick, but I am not yet incapable of coming downstairs."

"What is the matter?"

"Why can't it be good? Every time something good happens, something worse happens."

"I do not know, baby." She hugged me. "Why don't we go find Hope—she has been worried about you all day—then we can go to dinner?"

Dinner was the first normal thing of the day. No one mentioned anything unpleasant. After dinner, I suggested that we all go swimming. Hope and I played for a while, then Elizabeth joined in, and I started getting tired so I sat on the edge.

"Mom, shouldn't they be on their way to bed? It is almost 10 p.m."

"I know, Ann, but Tanya is not going to be up for playing for a while; let her have her fun."

"She is going to be fine; they will do another transplant if they have to."

"I know. I just don't want to see her go through it again. And on top of everything, the Johnsons called today and demanded another visitation with her."

"What did you tell them?"

"That is was not a good time. They are going to find out, but I do not want to deal with that right now."

I did not mean to be listening but I could not help myself. I walked over to the table and picked up my drink.

"How are you doing?"

"Fine."

"You look tired."

"Mom, I am fine."

"I know you; you are tired. I think it is time for bed." She walked me to my room; Emily was putting some new pajamas into a suitcase.

"Mom, I don't want this."

She smiled at me. "Well, do you want to wear a hospital gown?"

"No."

"Then you are going to have to put up with this, now go change."

When I came out of the bathroom, Emily was waiting with some more pills. I took them from her and then got into bed.

"Thank you, Emily. I am going to stay with her for a while." Emily smiled and left; then Mom sat next to me.

"Am I going to be as sick as I was last time?"

"Yes, baby."

I closed my eyes and laid my head on her lap; that is how I fell asleep. She woke me up in the morning and said it was time to go to the hospital. Hope and I hugged; Mom had to pull us apart. They admitted me into a private room and started the chemo right away.

I woke up, and Mom was reading a book. "Good morning. You have been asleep for a long time; do you think you are up to eating something?"

"No food."

"All right."

"Can I work on my homework?"

"Sure." She brought over some books and put them on the tray. The nurse brought in my lunch, and I ran for the bathroom. Mom was right behind me. After about ten minutes, I returned to bed. She got a cold washcloth and put it on my head. I fell asleep again. Hope came in the afternoon and we played cards. This routine continued every day. Mom was with me whenever I was sick; she held me and would rock me to sleep afterward. Nine days later, I was released from the hospital. I was weak and had no appetite, but Hope and I focused on the cruise.

Chapter Sixteen

We were leaving the following Saturday, staying a night in Miami, and then setting sail on Sunday. We had a two-bedroom suite for Hope and I to share with Mom and Craig; Elizabeth wanted her own room, so they decided to have her and Emily share. Ann and Chris, and Kate and Scott, each got their own rooms.

The ship was very large and elegant. After we set sail, Hope and I were out for some fun! We found everything possible to do! When we returned to our room, Mom was not too happy.

"Where have you two been?"

"At a get-to-know-you party in the teen dance room."

"It is 11."

"We know, that is why we came back; the party is still going on."

"All right, from now on, we will discuss what time you are to be back."

"Okay."

"Good, now go to bed. Tanya, come take your pills."

"I hate those things."

"Yes, but they are good for you."

The only time Hope and I were around was at dinner or when we were at port; the rest of the time we were out running around. We met a group of kids our age, and we hung out with them most of the time. They got a kick out of us being "twins." I had the time of my life! The last evening of the cruise, there was a midnight buffet and a teen dance. Two of the boys had asked us to go.

"You are not going on dates; you two are to young. No dating until you are sixteen, and you both know that."

"Dad, it is not like we are going to see them again; everyone goes home tomorrow."

"Hope, you know the rules, no exceptions. You may accompany your mother and I to the buffet."

"Can't Hope and I have one more night of fun before we go back home to everything? Please. Dad?" I gave him my sad eyes.

"Kerstin, your daughter is trying to manipulate me, and I think it is working."

Mom started laughing. "She must be good; you have survived her older five sisters. If I were you, I would just accept defeat."

He waved his hand and said fine. We both gave him a hug then ran to our room to change.

"Why did you give in so easily? NO matter how hard any of the girls begged, you have never bent the rules."

"She is our baby. In two days, she will be back in a hospital bed, living a life with cancer; let the child have fun."

When we arrived at the manor, the Johnsons' car was sitting outside. We pulled up to the house and they followed.

"We have been trying to get a hold of you for a week; we wanted to see Tanya for the holiday."

"We took the girls on a vacation."

"Well, it was nice of you to inform us."

"I am sorry, we did not realize that we had to inform you when we take our children someplace."

"She is not going to be yours much longer; we are appealing."

"All right! That is enough. I have tried to tell you that I am happy here, but you will not listen, so listen to this: I have leukemia and you are not helping."

Their faces went white and they turned to me. "What are you talking about? Have they brainwashed you to say that?"

"I have not been brainwashed. And if I were still living with you, I would be dead already. I have already received one transplant from Hope. I was meant to come back here so I could live."

"I do not believe you."

"Fine, follow me." They all followed me up to my room; I opened the doors and walked in. "Look around, my medication's on the table. My suitcase with all of my pajamas for when I go back to the hospital this week. Then there is Emily, my nurse."

"Oh, Tanya, if I had known I would have been here."

"My mom has been here with me through everything. And Dad arranges anything I need. I like being here."

"How long have you known?"

"A little over a year."

"You knew when you were home last March?"

"Yes, but I was in remission."

"You did not say anything."

"Mrs. Johnson, Tanya does not like being reminded of it; she wants a normal life, and so that is what we try and give her."

"Oh."

"If I show you what my life is like here, will you listen?"

"Yes, of course."

I walked over to my desk. "We are being home schooled right now; however, Hope and I have been accepted to the Premier Academy for next term. We each have our own teacher right now." I led them to the living room and sat down at the piano and played. I stopped and turned around. "Mom talked me into giving the piano another chance; she said that you could have fun when you are not being yelled at, and it is true. Every Sunday is family brunch; it lasts about the whole day, and every night dinner is in the dining room. Everyone attends unless Dad is having his associates over and we beg to eat upstairs. Once a week after dinner, Mom and Dad will find an activity for us all to partake in. We do go to New York and London, but that is fun! They are so different from here. They do spoil me, but they are also very strict. If I do not get all A's, then I start to lose privileges, and I have been grounded more times than I can count. They love me very much, and I love them. Just because I love them does not mean that I do not love you anymore. I tried telling you this in court, but you still did not listen. I alone decided to sever ties; I could not listen anymore to what you said about them."

Liz started crying. "I am sorry, we did not know how we were hurting you. We assumed what we have been saying because Craig is always in the news. And how can a family cope with all that and give six children the time they deserve? We are sorry we assumed wrong. I do see this is a good place for Tanya."

"Thank you. We do love her very much," Mom said, wrapping her arms around me.

"We will drop the appeal, but we do not want to lose her. Mrs. Delecroie, may we see her often?"

"I am not sure how often she will be able to come up, but we will try."

"Oh, I forgot you do not know. Jeff was transferred to a larger branch; we just moved to Santa Anna."

I looked up at them. "You live here?"

"Yes, we just finished the move last week."

Mom looked down at me and then at them. "Why don't you give us your address, and we will plan on Saturday? I cannot make any guarantees, though; it depends on how she feels. She will only be out of the hospital on Friday."

"That is great, thank you. May we come to the hospital?"

Mom looked down at me again and saw the look of panic in my eyes. "No, I am sorry. She is not allowed visitors because of the germs. I spend the days with her, and Hope is allowed because of their connection, but that is all the doctors will allow."

I walked over and gave them both a hug. "Thank you for finally listening."

They left and I felt relieved that it was over, no more fighting on where I would live. Mom went into the study and I followed her.

"Baby, what is wrong?"

"How much longer do I have to do this?"

"The doctor is going to run some more tests on Friday, then we will have a better idea." I nodded and looked down at the floor. She came over and knelt on the floor in front of me. "I know that this sucks. Everything always seems to happen to you, and it is not fair. You are strong, and we will get through this. I promise. When it is all over, we will go on a shopping spree, you, Hope, and me. Anywhere you want to go. We will just look forward to that, okay?"

"Okay."

She gave me a hug and then stood up. "You need to go get ready for bed; you have another big day tomorrow and you want to be rested for it."

This time, I got sick on the first morning. It was worse than before. By the third day, I did not even want to play cards with Hope. Mom called and told them not to even bring her here, that I was only sleeping all day. On Friday morning, she came in and woke me up in the morning.

"Tanya, you need to get up and get dressed."

"Mom…"

She handed me a lounging outfit. "Put this on and you will feel better."

"I don't feel good; I just want to sleep."

"After your appointment, I will take you home and you may sleep all weekend."

I did change with her help, then I sat down in the wheelchair, and she pushed me through the hospital and down to the office side. The doctor could tell that I was not feeling well and promised to make it is quick as possible so Mom could get me home. He drew my blood as well as his other tests that he did. Then he said he was going to the lab to get the results. I lay back and closed my eyes. I woke up when I heard the door open. I glanced at the clock and saw that he had been gone about 30 minutes.

"Mrs. Delecroie, Tanya, I believe that you have a guardian angel watching over you. I checked the results twice; however, the preliminary results show that Tanya is back in remission."

Mom hugged me. "That is wonderful!"

"Does this mean that I am done with the chemo?"

"No, one more treatment, and regular checkups for a while; we want to make sure that this time it does not come back."

When we got home, I went right to bed. Mom said that we could celebrate later. Hope woke me up in the early afternoon.

"Why did you not tell me?"

"I wanted to sleep," I said and hit her with my pillow. She grabbed another pillow and started hitting me back. Before we knew it, Elizabeth had come in, and the three of us had a pillow fight. Since I was feeling better, we went to dinner at a place overlooking the ocean. Mom even let us all have ice cream on the boardwalk.

"Feeling better, Tanya?"

"I will be after next week."

"I know, I will be also. Do you want to visit the Johnsons tomorrow?"

"Yes, I would like to give it another chance."

She tossed me her cell phone. "Why don't you call them and tell them that I will drop you off at 10 a.m.?"

Chapter Seventeen

The limo pulled up in front of a two-story house. As I got out of the car, Sam met me.

"Tanya!"

I turned in time for her to give me a hug. Mom got out of the car and handed me a purse. "Your phone is in here; call me when you are ready, all right?"

I gave her a kiss and then ran up to the house with Sam. Liz, Jeff, and Isabelle were inside; I gave them each a hug.

"Well, why don't we start by giving you a tour of our new house?"

The first floor consisted of a living room, dining room, kitchen, family room, and a den; the upstairs was the bedrooms. The first was a master bedroom with a bathroom; Sam's room was done in yellow and had posters all over the walls. Isabelle's was done in pink and covered in dolls and stuffed animals.

"Tanya, if you decided to stay overnight here at all, this is your room." Liz opened the door, and the room was done in purple and had all of my old things decorating the room.

"Tanya, I am sorry I cannot hang out longer but I have a ton of homework to do—the joy of starting a new school just before exams."

"I can help you, Sam."

"I am not sure, Tanya; it is high school work."

"Why don't we give it a shot?" I said, smiling at her. We went to the kitchen and opened her books on the table.

After about an hour, Sam looked up at me. "Tanya, how do you know all of this? You had to have your teeth pulled in order to pay attention in school."

"I was a bad student because I was bored but I still got the A's. Actually, we covered this material last spring at the Buchanan Academy."

"But you were only in seventh grade."

"Sam, it is a prep school. The parents expect that their daughters receive a first-class education in order to attend Ivy League schools. Their standards have to be better than a public school or they would lose many of their students."

"You have a good point. How did you do in that atmosphere?"

"I was top of my class."

"Oh." Sam and I continued to work on her homework for a while; then my phone rang.

"Hi, Mom!"

"Tanya, it is almost 6 p.m., and I have not heard from you. Are you doing all right?"

"Yes, I am fine; I am helping Sam with her homework."

"Do you want me to come and get you?"

"Can I have dinner over here?"

"Sure, just please do not overdo it. I will be by to get you around 8 p.m."

"Okay."

"I love you."

"Love you too." Sam and I picked up her books and put them away, then we went into the dining room.

"Mom, Tanya helped me finish all of my work. She did all this in seventh grade, and she got all A's."

"Wow, I was not aware of that."

We had pizza for dinner, and then we all went into the family room and played a board game. Mom picked me up at 8 p.m.

"Did you have a good time?"

"Yes, it was like old times."

"Good, I am glad. When we get home, it is straight to bed with you."

"But Mom, it will not even be 9 p.m. yet."

"Are you really going to try and argue with me?"

I looked down at my lap. "No. How about when we get home, I get ready for bed, and then Hope and I hang out for a while?"

"Lights out at 9:30 p.m."

"Thank you."

The manor had been decorated for the holidays while I was gone. I ran up the stairs to my room, and Hope came in. I told her about my day, and she told me about hers.

"Young Lady, why are you not in your pajamas?"

"Oh, sorry, we got carried away."

She came over and kissed the top of both of our heads.

"Well, it is time for you two to go to bed anyways. Hope, go get ready. I will be in shortly." She got up and walked out. "Okay, little one, to bed; this weekend is big, and I do not want you to overdo it."

"Okay."

By the time Sunday evening rolled around, I was exhausted. I excused myself early and went to bed. Mom decided to keep Emily on as a nanny for Hope and I. I think she felt better having a nurse around. The last week of chemo was the worst, but I looked forward to knowing that it was going to be over with. I slept the whole weekend. Ann and Chris came home for dinner on Sunday. Before dessert was served, Mom finally asked Ann what was wrong.

"Mom, nothing. Everything is fine."

"Ann, I know better. You have not said three words all night, and there is something wrong."

She looked at Chris and then back at Mom. "I am pregnant."

We all stopped and stared at her. Dad pushed his chair back and stood up. "You knew that I did not want you moving out without being married, and now you are pregnant! What were you thinking?"

"I am sorry."

"First, you are moving back into this house; second, you two better decide real fast about how you feel about each other."

"I know, Daddy, I am sorry."

"Sir, if you will allow me to, I would love to marry your daughter."

"Good. We will go to New York after Christmas and have a small ceremony with Chris's family, and then you two may announce the upcoming child."

"Thank you, Dad."

"You are still moving back into this house, tonight; after the marriage is final, the two of you will have a home here."

"Thank you, Mr. Delecroie."

"Chris, you are going to be part of this family. Call me Craig."

"Yes, sir."

That night, Ann was back in the house, and Mom came to the realization that she was going to be a grandmother. "I am too young to be a grandmother; I am not even fifty. I have two fourteen-year-old daughters. Annie, what are you trying to do to me?"

"Hey, it is your own fault for having children so young."

"I knew it was always possible."

"So, Hope, Tanya, you are going to be aunts."

Hope and I looked at each other. "We are not your built-in babysitters."

"Darn it. Oh well, I am not sure that I could count on you two anyways. I mean, look, Mom just hired you two a nanny."

"Emily is not a nanny; she is just here to help."

"Help do what? And two girls that have a nanny cannot be in charge of a baby."

"Ann, quit teasing your sisters; you know that Emily is here to ease my mind in case one of them has a relapse or something."

"I know, I am sorry."

"Girls, enough excitement for one day, Time for bed, and that includes you, Elizabeth. Ann, you should also go get ready; you need your rest now."

"Oh great, I am being sent to bed at the same time as two fourteen-year-olds."

"Well, get used to it darling. Now go."

I got ready for bed and Mom came in.

"All right, you wanted a heads up, so I had to move your checkup to tomorrow."

"No! Can't we wait til after Christmas?"

"Sorry, baby, we are going to New York. You may thank your sister for that."

"Well, we can wait til after we get back."

"You have one then also; however, you are going tomorrow. Hmm." She put her hand on my forehead. "You gave up too easily."

"There is no point in arguing, is there?"

"No, however, it is not like you to give up so easily."

"You are just doing what is best for me. I know that you do not want to lose me; I know why because I really miss Sara." I started crying.

She reached over and pulled me in to her. "I know. I miss her so much. I know that she is still here with us. She is your guardian angel, why you went back into remission so fast, and they said if you had a relapse, there was probably going to be nothing they could do. She is Hope's guardian angel also; the doctors said that she probably would not walk again, and look at her. Six months later and you can hardly tell that there was a problem. That is how I know that Sara is still with us; I see her every time I look at you and when I look at Hope." I fell asleep with her holding me.

The next few days went very fast. On Christmas Eve, Mom took me over to the Johnsons for a short visit. Christmas morning, Hope woke me up, and we both went in to get Mom and Dad up. Then we took off to the living room. The tree was piled high with presents; however, now it did not phase me. We both received several new outfits, some new formal wear, books, DVDs and a PDA. Among several other things.

After Christmas morning, we all got ready to go to New York. We arrived at the Penthouse around midnight. Hope and I went to my room and fell asleep. When we woke up, the place was filled with noise.

"Morning, girls. Did you sleep well?"

"Yes."

"Good. I put an outfit for you both in the bathroom. Breakfast is about ready, and then we are going to get the dresses fitted. I have a few other things to get ready also. Tomorrow, we are going upstate and we will visit the country club. Then the wedding will be the following day. Now get changed; Chris's parents are here."

We changed into the outfits set out for us: white blouses, knee-length skirts, knee-high socks, and headbands.We entered the dining room; everyone was already there.

"Rose, Edward, may I introduce you to my youngest daughters, Hope and Tanya. Girls, this is Mr. and Mrs. Gilmore."

"It is nice to meet you, Mrs. and Mr. Gilmore," we replied in unison.

"Kerstin, they are so cute and well mannered; you must be so proud."

"Yes, I am. Thank you."

"Mom, I have a headache. May I please pass on breakfast?" She was next to me in seconds and had her hand on my forehead. "Mom, it is just a headache, a take-two-aspirin type thing."

"You are not warm, but go lie down. Emily will bring you some aspirin, and I will check on you after a while." She kissed the top of my head, and I went back to my room. I really only wanted some alone time. Emily appeared with the aspirin and then left. I watched television for a while, and then Mom appeared.

"Well, if you are watching television, you must be feeling better?"

"Yes, a bit."

"Good. Let's get going; we have a big day, lots of things to accomplish." I got up and followed her out of the room.

We were fitted for our dresses. Kate, Elizabeth, Hope, and I all had pale pink dresses, while Ann's dress was white silk with a long train. It was after 9 when we returned to the penthouse. Hope slept in my room again; neither one of us wanted to go into her room. The door had remained shut since we had arrived. Mom understood where we were coming from and decided that Hope would be moved into Ann's old room. Ann and Chris received the apartment downstairs next to Kate's. In the morning, we took the plane upstate to go to the country club where the wedding was going to be. All the preparations were well underway.

"Ann, tell Chris goodbye; he will be returning back to his parents, and you will see him tomorrow."

"Mom. Chris and I were going to spend this evening together."

"Not a chance. You are staying with us, and he will stay with his parents. Go say goodbye."

"Mom, Chris and I just…"

"Do not argue. I am still your mother, and you will still do as I tell you. Now go say goodbye. Girls, come, we are leaving." Hope and I were laughing; it was funny watching Ann being told what to do.

The ceremony went well, as did the reception. We all flew back to New York City after the reception, and then Ann and Chris flew to London for their honeymoon. While we were gone, Hope had officially been moved into her new room.

"Girls, to bed. It is late, and you have had a big few days." I said goodnight to Hope and Mom and returned to my room. I emailed Keri and then Sam; then I had a hand fall onto my shoulder.

"Do I need to take the computer away?"

I turned and looked up at Mom. "No, I am sorry."

"I sent you to bed over an hour ago. You have not even changed into your pajamas yet. Now turn off the computer and go change."

"Mom, don't you think we are getting a little old for a bedtime?"

"No, but you are lucky; when Kate was your age, she still went to bed at

8:30 p.m."

"Why?"

"I had four children under the age of 5. I needed some peace."

I crawled into bed and she sat down next to me. "All right, little one, tomorrow you are in bed at 8:30 p.m."

"But Mom."

"Hey, you disobeyed me; your father would take away the computer."

"Fine."

"Goodnight." She kissed my head and then left the room.

Chapter Eighteen

Mom wanted to go back to California for New Years; however, Dad wanted to stay in New York City so he could check on some business. Elizabeth spent the time catching up with her friends, Mom set up meetings, and Hope and I hung out with Kate. On New Years eve, Mom and Dad were planning on going to a party, Kate and William were going with them, and Emily went back to California for some time off, so Hope, Elizabeth, and I were staying home.

"Remember that you stay in the apartment. You may stay up and watch the ball drop, then off to bed. I will call and check on you."

"Okay."

She gave us each a hug and then left. Elizabeth looked at us. "When they call, tell them I am in the bathroom or in bed."

"Lizzy, where are you going?"

"Hope, don't worry about it."

"Liz, do you want us to cover for you?"

"Fine. Mary Ann is having a party; I will be back before they get home."

"Why did you not just ask?"

"I did. Mom said no." She left.

Hope and I watched videos and played games. We cleaned up our mess just before midnight. Just as we were finishing, the phone rang.

"Happy New Year, Tanya."

"Happy New Year."

"Is everything going all right?"

"Yes."

"Let me talk to Elizabeth."

"Elizabeth?" I looked at Hope. "I think she is in bed."

"Oh, all right. We will be home in a while. I love you all."

"Love you too." I hung up and looked back at Hope "Where is she?"

"I do not know; let's call her cell phone." We did, but there was no answer.

An hour went by and she still was not back. The door opened; we both turned, and to our dismay, it was our parents.

"Hi, girls. Why are you not in bed?"

"Sorry, we are going." We both jumped up and started running toward our rooms.

"Freeze." We both stopped and slowly turned around. "Why are you two so quick to leave? You did not even come give me a hug." Hope and I looked at each other.

"Kerstin, I just looked in on Elizabeth; her room is empty." They both turned to us. "Hope Victoria, Tanya Alexandra, living room, now!"

We quickly moved back down the hall and entered the living room.

"Sit down." We did quickly. "I am going to ask you this once and I want an answer. Where is your sister?"

Just then Elizabeth appeared in the door. He turned to her. "Elizabeth Samantha, sit down. Where have you been?"

"I went to the party."

"You two knew about this?"

"Yes, sir," we replied.

"And you lied to your mother?"

"Yes, sir."

"Hope, follow me. You two, do not move." They left the room. About 10 minutes later, they returned. Hope was not with them.

"I am not sure which one of you I should be more disappointed in. You both lied and deceived us."

"Daddy, Tanya was…"

"Elizabeth, do not try the Daddy's-little-girl thing with me, and Tanya knew there would be trouble if you got caught. Now, Hope has received her punishment and is now in bed. You both are on restriction—Elizabeth, six months, and Tanya, three months. This includes no credit cards, cell phones, allowances. Elizabeth, your car is gone. No television, computers are for schoolwork only, no movies or shows, regular phone by approval only. No friends over. No after-school activities including dances, field hockey, and soccer. You will go to bed after dinner. When you get home from school, you will report to your mother or me and be supervised until dinner. Weekends will be similar. You may earn back some privileges by doing what you are told, and no complaints. Understand?"

"Yes, sir."

"Any questions?"

"No, sir."

"Good. Now go to bed and do not ever pull a stunt like that again."

We got up. I gave Mom a hug and then turned toward my room.

"Tanya, I am sorry."

"Are you sorry you went or are you sorry you got caught, and all of us in trouble?"

"All of it. I am sorry."

Mom woke me up at 6 a.m. the next morning. "We are going back to California; please be ready in forty minutes."

"Mom, I am sorry."

"I know you are, baby."

The flight was boring since none of us were allowed to do anything. Dad actually made us each write a report on the dangers of sneaking out and lying to your parents. When we got home, we were all sent to our rooms. My television had already been taken away, and my computer had a password lock on it. Emily came in a short time later.

"All right, what did you guys do? You come home from vacation and you are all sent to your rooms."

"Liz snuck out, and we covered for her."

"Ouch, so what is the sentence?"

"Hope is three weeks, I have three months, and Liz is six months."

"Wow, that is a long time. Are you mad at your parents?"

"No, I am mad at myself for covering for Liz, and I am mad at Liz for asking me to do so."

"Are you ever going to do so again?"

"Not a chance."

"So your parents got their message through?"

"Loud and clear.

"Good, little one. I am glad that you understand you have to pay for your actions."

"Hello, Mom. Yes, I do."

She kissed my forehead. "Dinner will be ready in a half hour."

"All right."

"Do not forget you are starting at the Premier Academy tomorrow."

"I know."

"Just remember your restrictions."

Hope and I both went to bed right after dinner. I was actually tired from lack of sleep the night before. The next morning, I changed into the school uniform and then I pulled my hair back into a ponytail. Mom took Hope and me to school. Elizabeth was upset that she had to ride with us because she could not drive her car. When we arrived at the school, it was different than I had expected. The lobby was filled with couches and had a fountain in the center.

"Girls, have a seat. I have a meeting with Mrs. Culver." She was gone about a half hour. Some students started coming through the lobby; they would smile and some said hi. Mom returned with a lady about the same age as her.

"Girls, this is Mrs. Culver. She is the principal here. This is Hope Victoria and Tanya Alexandra Delecroie."

"Good morning, ma'am."

"Good morning, girls. I think you are going to like it here."

"Girls, Anthony will pick you up this afternoon. Tanya, you are to come to my office when you get home."

I nodded at her. The Premier academy was styled a lot like the Buchanan Academy with their class styles.

This school was a boarding school, but also had several day students. The campus was large. Hope and I had homeroom, lunch, and last hour together. Everything else, we were separated.

"We like to have siblings separated so they may become acquainted with other students. However, we do realize that you two do need to be together a bit."

My Schedule was as follows:

English
French
American Government
American Justice System
Advanced Algebra
Music Appreciation

Hope's was:

French
English
Biology
Geometry
Chemistry
Music Appreciation

When I walked into third hour, people were calling me Hope. "I am Tanya. Hope is my sister."

"Oh, people must get you confused all of the time."

"No, not really; they either know us very well or they have figured out our father's way to tell us apart."

"How is that?"

"My things are purple; Hope's are pink."

"That is funny. Have you ever switched?"

"No, our mother knows us too well; she knows which one of us has entered a room without even looking at us."

"Wow, my Mom can't even do that, and I am an only child. Is it just the two of you?"

"No, I have five sisters."

"Your house must be fun."

"Sometimes."

"Your sister and you should come over to my house sometime."

"I would love to; however, I am grounded for the next three months."

"Ouch, what did you do?"

"I covered for my sister who snuck out in New York City and did not come home til after 1 a.m."

"Three months is a long time."

"My parents are a little strict."

"I see. At least they are aware of what you do. By the way, my name is Marci."

I was thrilled to see Hope at lunch; we ate at a table by ourselves and then we had go back to class. By the time the day was over, I was glad. I had homework from every class. The car was waiting for us as we exited the building; I went straight to Mom's office when we arrived home.

"Hello, Tanya. How was school?"

"Fine. I have an awful lot of classes pertaining to government and the laws."

"Your scholastic aptitude test showed that you would do well in a career in law. I told you to start thinking about a career."

"Mom, I am fourteen."

"Yes, and in four years you will be going to college."

"Four years?"

"Sooner if you go into the accelerated program."

"I did not realize that it was coming up so soon. I mean, that is like next week," I said sarcastically.

She ignored my tone and continued. "Do you think that you will like law?"

"I am not sure. I guess it cannot hurt to give it a try."

"Have a seat and start your homework."

I finished my homework by five thirty. I closed my books and put them back into my bag. Mom looked at me from her desk.

"Did you double-check your work?"

"Yes."

"Let me see your French." I opened my folder and handed it to her. "This is very good. I am almost done; why don't you get a book, and then we can go see how your sister is faring with your father?"

I opened my bag and pulled out my book; she looked down at it, then at me. "Book report, due in three weeks."

"Fiction or nonfiction?"

"Fiction. Next one is nonfiction."

"Good. Did you enjoy yourself?"

"Yes, I had fun for the most part. I also met a girl, Marci," I said as we walked toward Dad's office. "She asked me to come over to her house."

"What did you tell her?"

"I told her I would love to, in three months."

She put her arm around me and smiled. "It sucks being grounded, huh?" She tapped on the door and then opened it. "Hello, Craig. Elizabeth, how was school?"

"All right."

"Are you finished with your homework?"

"Almost."

"Sweetie, what is wrong?"

"I have a bedtime the same as a fourteen-year-old, and I am not allowed to drive nor do anything without a chaperone until after my graduation! What do you think is wrong?"

"Elizabeth Samantha Delecroie, you do not speak to your mother that way. If you would like more respect from us, then you need to show us some respect in return. Look at your sister. Your stunt got her in just as much trouble as you, and she is not sitting here complaining. Now apologize to your mother."

"I am sorry."

"Good, now sit down and finish your homework. Tanya, how was your first day at Premier?"

"Good. I enjoyed it."

"I am glad."

"Baby, why don't you read for a little bit? Your father and I have some business to discuss."

I retreated to the couch and read for a while. When they were through talking, we went to the dining room for dinner. We were all sent to our rooms to get ready for bed when dinner was over. I was getting into bed when there was a knock on the door.

"Come in."

The door opened and Dad appeared. I was almost shocked; he never came into my room. "Are you ready for bed?"

"Yes."

"Here," he said, pulling a book from his jacket. "You left this in my office. Your mother said that it is for a book report?"

"Yes, I thought it might be interesting," I said, taking the book from him.

"You may read for an hour. Lights out at 8:30."

"Thank you."

"You are welcome. Your mother will be back up in a little while. Goodnight"

"Goodnight, Dad."

The next few weeks went the same way. Hope was released from restriction, Ann and Chris came home from their honeymoon, and Ann's pregnancy became public knowledge. I was given back a few privileges. I no longer was required to report to Mom's office when I got home; however, I continued to do so. I enjoyed spending some time with her. My grades continued to be excellent, and I did everything I was told. I even quit complaining about my checkups. In the end of February, they announced soccer tryouts during our lunch period.

"Tanya, you should try out; you are really good."

"Marci, I am still grounded."

"Can't you ask?"

"Tanya, Dad specifically said no soccer."

"I know." But I did really want to play. Sixth hour was cut short so we could go get our progress reports from our homerooms. When we got home, Ann met us at the door. "Hope, you and I are going shopping. Tanya, Mom is on her way down."

"Way down for what?"

"I am sorry, baby. I had to reschedule your checkup," she said as she came down the stairs.

I looked at her and shrugged. "All right."

She gave me a concerned look and then waved me toward the car. "I have to go to London next week for some meetings. You and Hope are going to be on spring vacation, so I am going to take you with me."

"Okay."

We entered the doctor's office, and I was led right into the exam room.

"Hello, Tanya, Mrs. Delecroie. How are you doing?"

"Fine."

"Tanya, is there anything out of the ordinary?

"No."

"Good, I am going to have to poke you some more today."

I hated doctors and I hated needles, two things that I had decided I hated the most. But I was not going to argue. "All right."

When we arrived back home, Hope and Ann were not back yet. I turned to go to my room.

"Tanya, what are you going to do?"

"Some projects."

"I did not know that you had any."

"Just a head start," I said and started up the stairs.

"Freeze right there."

I turned around and looked at her. "Yes?"

She walked over to the library and opened the doors. "In here." I walked back down and entered the room. "Have a seat." I sat on the couch, and she sat down on the coffee table across from me. "You have not complained about anything, and I know you hate the doctor and the needles. Also, you have not said more than thirteen words all afternoon. What is wrong?"

"Nothing. Everything is wonderful."

"Then why are you not acting like yourself?"

"No particular reason," I said and looked at her. She did not budge, just stared at me. I broke. "It is just…"

"Tanya, what?"

"Soccer tryouts are this week."

"You are still on restriction."

"I know, I was just hoping maybe…"

"How badly do you want it?"

"Very."

"Well, your father is the one that has to give you permission. He is a businessman and he thrives on compromise; you are a bright kid so you figure it out."

"I need to give him something he deems worthwhile."

"Gosh, you are smart, another trait you must have gotten from your mother."

"Ha!" I smiled at her. "What does he want?"

"He wants you to be happy, but he really would like to have his baby girl and know her."

I took a deep breath and looked at her. "Is he in his office?"

"Yes."

I gave her a hug. "Thank you."

I knocked on his door and stuck my head in "May I come in?"

"Yes, Hope." I opened the door and walked in. "Tanya?"

"I just wanted to come up and say hi."

"Thank you. How was school?"

"Good. I am enjoying it."

"Good. Are you still interested in the law classes?"

"Yes, sir, I am."

"Good. Someday my eldest daughter and youngest daughter will be working with me at Delecroie Enterprises."

"Really?"

"I would love it."

"I never thought about that."

"Well, if you are still considering law, I could use you, so please do."

"I have a project in American justice; do you have any ideas on topics?"

"Yes, I could help you if you would like."

"That would be great."

He came around the desk and gave me a hug. "How did your appointment go?"

"Fine. They took more blood than usual."

"Did you drink enough juice?"

"Yes, Mom would not leave me alone until she was satisfied."

"Good. She really loves you."

"I know."

"So what else did you do at school today?"

"Not much. I read a bit at lunch; all of my friends are getting ready for soccer tryouts."

"What was Hope doing?"

"Going to a swim meeting."

"I see. How are your grades?"

"Good. We received out reports today."

"Do you have it with you?"

"Yes." I opened my bag and pulled it out.

"I do not see how they can get better than this. Is it because of interest or boredom?"

"Interest."

"Do you want to play soccer?"

"Of course I do."

"Do not make me regret this: You may try out."

"Thank you!" I gave him a hug.

He smiled. "You are welcome. Why don't you go find your sister? Dinner will be ready shortly."

I walked out of his office and ran toward the living room. Hope was reading her book on the couch. "Hope, he said that I could try out!"

She looked up at me, confused. "How did you pull that off? He never gives in on things like that."

"I don't know. We were just talking about it, and he asked if I wanted to play, I said yes, and he told me I could try out!"

"That is great! Marci will be happy."

"I know!"

The next day, I tried out and made the starting team! Hope made the swim team's new elite team also! They gave us a schedule; practices were going to start as soon as spring break was over.

Chapter Nineteen

Elizabeth did not have the same spring break as us, so she was staying home with Dad while Hope and I went with Mom to London. On the flight, Mom let me watch some movies; however, when we arrived in London, she reminded me of my restrictions, which now were only no television, phone, or allowance. The first night Mom took us out to dinner, and then she warned us that she would be working most of the time here. We were to be on our best behavior and we were not allowed to leave the property. She was true to her word; she barely made it home in time for dinner each night. Hope and I did not leave the property again until we left to go back to California.

The first day back to school, I was excited when the final bell rang. It was the first day of soccer practice; while I was there, Hope was going to swim practice. It became my routine: When I got home, I would stop by Mom's office to say hi, then go to Dad's to discuss my project. He was actually giving me a lot of help, and the project was my final. Then I would go finish the rest of my homework and meet the family for dinner. Mom came to my room every night to talk for a few minutes. On April 2nd, my television was returned to my room, as well as my phone. Mom gave me back my credit cards and my cell phone. In mid April, I had my first soccer game. Mom, Dad, Liz, and Jeff all came, as well as Ann, Elizabeth, Hope, Sam, and Isabelle. I made three goals, including the winning goal. Everyone enthusiastically met me after the game.

"Tanya, we are so proud of you!"

"Thank you!" I said, giving Mom and Dad both a hug.

"Mrs. Delecroie, we would like to take Tanya out to celebrate."

Mom and Dad looked at each other. "It is already getting late."

"If you do not mind, we could keep her overnight; we have a room for her."

I watched Mom and Dad; they were both silent for a while looking at each other. Then Mom nodded her head. "We will send a car for her at noon tomorrow."

I gave them and Hope a hug, then left with the Johnsons. We went out for pizza and then went back to their house. Mom had already sent some clothes over for me. I changed into my pajamas and fell asleep right away.

"Wake up." There was a hand over my mouth; I opened my eyes to see a masked man standing over me. "You are coming with me. If you do not fight me, you will not get hurt." He then waved a gun in front of me. He grabbed my wrist, keeping his other hand tightly over my wrist. "Let's go."

He pulled me out of the window and threw me into the back of a van. The windows were blacked out. The van started to move, and then the air started to smell funny. I woke up in a room on a cot. There were no windows and no other furniture. The door opened, and the same man entered carrying a tray of food. "Hungry?"

"I want to go home."

"Soon enough."

"Where am I"?

"Do not worry about it."

"Why am I here?"

"Do not worry about it."

"I WANT TO GO HOME!"

"As soon as your father pays up, you can go home."

"My father?"

"Yes, we have been watching you and that sister of yours, just waiting for a chance. Now eat or not; hopefully you will not be here long." He turned and left. I followed over to the door, but it was locked.

This was the Delecroie curse, I decided. Every time life got going well, the floor dropped out. I curled up on the cot. How long had I been gone? Where was I? Hours passed; no one came back. After a while, the lights went out. I must have fallen asleep again because I woke up again when the man came back in.

"No more food. We are not wasting it. When you eat that, you can have more."

"I want to go home," I said calmly.

"Soon." He turned and left again.

I found my way back to my safe place in my head: the neverland I had escaped from last August. I was unaware of my surroundings. After several more hours, he came back, grabbed me, and threw me back into that van. We drove for a while and then we stopped.

"GET OUT." I did, quickly. "Sit down and count to 100. Do not move until you get there."

I sat on the grass and waited. The car pulled away, and the plates were covered. It was dark, late evening or early morning. After a few moments, I got up and started walking; about a quarter mile away was a house. I went up to it and rang the bell.

An elderly lady opened the door and gasped. "You are the missing Delecroie girl."

I did not say a thing. She took my hand and pulled my inside; then she got a blanket and wrapped it around me. Shortly the house was swarming with police.

They took me to the hospital; doctors, nurses, and police were all around me asking me questions. I did not say a word. Shortly after we arrived at the hospital, the door opened; Mom and Dad appeared. They both ran over to me and put their arms around me.

"Baby, are you okay?" I looked up at her and started crying. She wrapped her arms around me again. "You are safe now; we will not let anything happen to you again."

"Doctor, is she physically okay?"

"Yes, Mr. Delecroie. A little dehydrated, and she probably has not eaten since she disappeared, but overall, she will be fine."

"When can we take her home?"

"Soon. We are concerned that she is not talking."

"She has done this before. Her mother brought her out of it last time. She quit speaking after the car accident that killed her sister. She has been through so much; I want to get her home where she will feel safe again."

"Mr. Delecroie, we still need to question the girl."

"I realize that, detective. However, if we get her home, she will relax a bit and maybe start speaking again. You are more than welcome to join us in our home when she is ready."

I wanted to go home so badly. I closed my eyes and laid my head in Mom's lap. She started brushing my hair with her hand.

"Mr. Delecroie, go ahead and take her home."

I opened my eyes and looked at him; he came over to me and put his jacket around me, then picked me up and carried me out of the room. In the limo, I put my head back on her lap and closed my eyes.

"Tanya, we are so happy you are okay. Your sisters have been so worried that they have not gone to school."

They have not gone to school? What day was it? My game had been Friday, so today should be Sunday. I opened my eyes; Mom was wearing her watch with the day on it also. I took her hand and looked at it. Tuesday. Four days, was it really four days?

"Baby, did you know how long you were gone?"

I shook my head. We pulled up to the gates. They were usually open, but now they were closed. They opened, then closed behind the car. When I got out of the car, I was bombarded by siblings. Kate, Ann, Elizabeth, Hope, Sam, and Isabelle were all there. They all gave me a hug, and then I went inside with Mom and Hope.

"Why don't we get you cleaned up, and then we will have lunch?"

I was starving, but I was still wearing my pajamas from Friday. She started my shower and then picked out an outfit for me. When I was changed, we went down to the dining room. Sam and Isabelle were still there.

"Sam, your parents are just now finishing up with the detectives at your house. They will be over shortly to get you guys."

"Thank you, Mr. Delecroie."

I sat down at the table and ate everything on my plate. Mom asked if I wanted some more, but I said no. After everyone was done, we all went into the rec room. Everyone played games, but I just watched. Liz and Jeff showed up and told me how sorry they were. When no one was watching, I quietly got up and retreated to my room. I was lying on my bed, curled up, when Mom came in.

"Baby, will you talk to me?" She sat down on the bed next to me. I started crying.

"I was scared."

She moved so my head was on her lap. "We were scarred too; my nightmare was happening all over again."

"He told me that if I did not fight, I would not be hurt. He had a gun, then he put me in a van, and it started to smell. I woke up in a bare room; there was not even a window. I wanted to come home. He said not until Dad paid him. A while later, he put me back in the van and left me on that road. He told me not to move. I was scared."

"I know you were, but you are safe now. And we are going to be more careful now. I promise. The detectives are in the hall; do you think you can talk to them?"

"Don't leave me."

Two men walked in. I sat up and moved over to the couch. They sat across from me.

"Tanya, this is a very nice room you have."

"Thank you."

"Do you remember whom the man was who took you?"

"No, he wore a mask. He had a deep voice."

"Where did he take you?"

"I don't know. The windows were blocked out. We drove for a while, I think."

"Thank you, Tanya. We are glad that you are home." They got up and left.

"I need to do my homework or I am going to fall behind."

"We have a few things to take care of before you go back to school; maybe we will go back to home school."

"No, Please don't. I want to stay at Premier."

"I know. We just need to make sure that they have their security up to par. We have been lax with your security since letting you go to the Johnsons without a guard."

"A guard?"

"Yes."

"I want to be normal, not have somebody following me around all the time."

"I want you to be safe; here you are safe. At school you will be safe. When you are somewhere that we cannot make sure you are safe, you will have a guard. This goes for your sisters as well."

"He said that he had been watching us."

"We know. He sent us pictures of you, Hope, and Elizabeth. That is when we realized that we need to change out security. I do not know what I would have done if something worse had happened to you." She gave me a hug.

"Why don't you rest?"

"Why were Sam and Isabelle here?"

"The police were swarming their house, so they have been staying here."

"Oh. I am going to work on my homework."

"Take your time. I think we will have you start back on Monday."

"I want to go back tomorrow, a normal life. Back to normal."

She looked at me for a few moments and then shook her head. "All right, I will go make some calls."

"Thank you. Actually, do you think I could go swimming?"

"Yes, go have fun."

I hugged her and ran down the hall. Elizabeth, Sam, and Isabelle joined me. We played for most of the afternoon. Liz and Jeff took Sam and Isabelle home. They invited me out the next weekend, but I declined; I did not want to go back to their house—ever.

Chapter Twenty

Mom dropped us off at school, and they welcomed me back, but no one said another thing. I was glad; I did not want to talk about it. I noticed that there was more staff around than usual. Between my soccer and Hope's swimming, we were spending most of our time at school or on schoolwork. Dad was excited that I was taking a real interest in law. My favorite was juvenile; however, I let him think it was corporate.

As May approached, Elizabeth was preparing for graduation. She still had no credit cards or allowance; however, everything else had been returned to her. She was very excited about going to college. She had decided to go to NYU; she missed New York City and wanted to go back. While she was preparing for graduation, Hope and I were getting ready for our exams. Mom had to make us break for dinner and then would tell us to stop and go to bed. The weekend before the finals, I spent the weekend in my room and studied constantly.

"Tanya, I have barely seen you all weekend."

"I have been studying. I want to get into the student justice program, but I have to have one of the top three grades."

"The internship program your senior year?"

"Yes, but we get selected this year, and then prep for it the next two years."

"Well, I know you will do your best." She leaned over and kissed my head. "I know you and Hope will have good futures; I just wish Elizabeth had it figured out."

"Has she decided what she wants to do?"

"Still produce."

"I thought Dad was against that?"

"He is. He knows that it is a hard field."

"Yeah, I can see that."

"Yeah? Who taught you this slang?"

"Sorry, Mom. I need to get back to studying."

"All right. I need to go check on Hope. Lights out in two hours; you do not want all of your studying to go to waste."

"All right."

"I love you."

"Love you too."

Monday morning, we started our exams. I had two exams a day for three days. When we got home on Wednesday, we were both exhausted; we both fell asleep in my room.

"They are still adorable when they are asleep. They look so peaceful."

"I know."

My eyes sprang open. Mom and Dad were both standing there watching us.

"How did your exams go?"

"I think I did all right."

"Me too," Hope said, opening her eyes.

"Well, you both did your best. That is all that matters. Do not worry about it."

"We won't."

Mom let us stay up later than normal, and we played games and went swimming.

Thursday morning, I was more nervous than I had been during the exams. After homeroom, the entire freshman class had to go to an assembly where they were going to announce the students going into the accelerated programs, along with other awards.

Hope and I received awards for the National Honor Society and Academic Excellence. Finally it came time for what we were waiting for.

"As you all know, this has been a critical year for all of you. Today nine of you will be selected to go into the accelerated programs for the area of interests you have chosen. There are three majors here, and each will receive three new students to continue in the accelerated programs for the remainder of their time here. When I call your name, please come onto the stage. First, our medical program: Jessica Heart, Vicki Long, and Hope Delecroie."

We hugged and she ran onto the stage.

"For our student justice program: Tanya Delecroie, Marci Jones, and Mari Cinder."

I ran onto the stage, and Hope and I hugged again! I was too excited to pay attention to the last three who were called for the business program. That concluded the awards ceremony. As we left the auditorium, everyone told us "congratulations." Then we returned to our homeroom to receive our schedules for the following year and our report cards for this year. I had:

English
General Education
English; Law Terminology
Justice System
Divisions of Law
Political Science

We walked out to the car, both excited.

"Jacob, may we please stop for ice cream on the way home?"

"I am sorry, Miss Hope; your parents are both busy and have requested that you be taken straight home."

"Please?"

"Miss Tanya, you know that I follow your parents' requests."

"What is so important?"

"They are preparing for your sister's graduation in addition to having a big meeting with their associates."

"Oh."

Emily met us at the door when we arrived. "How did it go?"

"Well! We both made it!"

"Your parents are going to be so proud of you! Now, you both need to go put your things away and change. Your mother just called; she is on her way to get you. You are going out to dinner with some of their associates."

"Wonderful! Just how I wanted to spent this evening."

"Tanya Alexandra, best behavior please."

I turned around to see Mom walking up. "Sorry, we were just hoping that since it is the last day of school…"

"Sorry, girls, you are going. These are very important people, and they are here for your sister's graduation."

"Why do we have to go?"

"Because I said so. Now let's get moving. You are fine in your uniforms." We followed her out to the car, and then she stopped and turned around. "Girls, I am sorry. How did your grades turn out?"

"We both got straight A's."

"Good." She paused, looking at us both closely. "And how about the other thing?"

"Mom, we both got in! We were both accepted."

"That is wonderful!" She pulled us both into a hug. "Wait until your father hears!"

We arrived at the restaurant; Dad was already there. He was with a man, a woman, and a girl about our age. He gave Mom a kiss, then looked at us.

"Hello, girls," he said and then he gave us each a hug.

"Hello, Father," we both replied in turn.

"Girls, this is Mr. and Mrs. Camden and their daughter Arial. These are my youngest, Hope and Tanya."

"It is very nice to meet you all."

"Kerstin, Craig, they are adorable, especially in their school uniforms. We have a hard time keeping Arial in a school let alone a uniform."

"Mom, just drop it."

"Kerstin, I have to hand it you. You raised six daughters and co-run Delecroie Enterprises. I have a hard time raising one."

"Thank you. I just developed a system and I stuck to it."

"You may have to write a book about it."

"Thank you again for allowing us to eat early. I am still not quite adjusted from the East Coast time."

"No problem."

At the table, I sat between Hope and Mom; Arial sat on the other side of Hope.

"Arial, are you on a vacation or is your term over?"

"Mrs. Delecroie, I am on an unscheduled vacation, you could say. Our term is not over until mid June."

"What grade are you in?"

"I will be completing the eighth grade."

"You are fourteen?"

"Yeah."

"If I remember correctly, you were born a month after Hope, Sara, and Tanya, in October?"

"Yes, she was. So, Hope, Tanya, how are you doing in school?"

We looked at each other.

"Ma'am, today was the last day of this term, and we both did quite well."

"That is right. Girls, hand over you reports."

We both pulled them out, leaving the letters attached.

"You were both accepted into the accelerated program! This is wonderful."

"Are they attending the Premier Academy?"

"Yes."

"That is an accelerated school program already. What grade are you girls in?"

"We will be entering grade 10 in the fall."

"Arial, see how much you could accomplish if you tried?"

"Blah, blah, blah." Arial acted like a spoiled brat. I may have been spoiled; however, if I acted like she did, I would not have been spoiled much longer.

Dinner went well, and then we returned to the manor where the preparations for the graduation party were coming along. The next day, we attended Elizabeth's graduation from St. Margaret's. After the ceremony, everyone came for the big party at the house. Hope and I were bored. We finally snuck away halfway through and went horseback riding. We were having so much fun on the trails that we lost track of time and did not head back til it was getting dark. We were talking as we walked the horses back into the stables.

"Hope Victoria, Tanya Alexandra, go to your rooms." Dad was standing in the door; he grabbed the reins out of our hands. His eyes meant business.

"Yes, sir." We both turned and quickly left.

"I have been getting in trouble a lot lately, and we did not do anything wrong this time."

"Yes, well, I am sure we will be told shortly what we did so wrong."

We saw no one as we entered the house. The party had been cleaned up and almost all evidence was gone. When we arrived at our rooms, we gave each other a hug and then went into our own room. I decided that I had better get ready for bed since it was getting late, and my punishment was usually being sent to bed. Mom was sitting on the end of my bed when I walked out of my bathroom.

"Mom, we did not mean to do anything wrong. I am really sorry."

"You did not do anything wrong. We had a scare at the party. There was a picture of you two, and across it was written 'Do you know where your children are?' We could not find you."

"Am I in danger again?"

"No, baby. It turns out that Arial decided that she did not want to be here, so she wanted to play a joke on us."

"So why did he use the middle names?"

"He overreacted. He was pretty upset."

"So what is going to happen to Arial?"

"A very nice reform school. Her parents said they could no longer control her, so they decided it was time. Her unscheduled vacation from school is actually from being expelled."

"Ouch."

"Yes, well, she has been expelled from four schools in the past year."

"Why?"

"She is selfish. Reform school will teach her a little about getting what she wants."

"What do you mean?"

"You have to be granted permission to use the restroom or to speak. Merits gain you privileges, demerits, you lose them. She will share a room with about 25 other students and work in the mess hall."

"I think I will pass on attending one."

She smiled at me. "Oh you do, do you?" Then she started tickling me; I started laughing. "I love it when you are laughing. I do not want to upset you; however, you do have a checkup tomorrow."

"On a Saturday?"

"Yes, but the sooner we get it over with and everything is good, the next one is not until August."

"All right."

While I had my appointment, Mom had also made a checkup for Ann. Then she took us out to lunch.

That summer, I started to study legal terminology. I wanted to be a step ahead when school started. Dad had fun quizzing me. Hope did the same and Ann quizzed her. Hope and I spent every other Saturday at the Johnsons. Hope and Sam got along wonderfully. August was looking to be an interesting month. Elizabeth was moving to New York, Ann would be having her baby, and Hope and I were entering the 10th grade at age 14. Sam thought it was awkward that we were now in the same grade.

Chapter Twenty-One

"Tanya, we are taking Ann to the hospital. Chris is on his way back from New York. We will call you in the morning."

"Okay. What time is it?"

"Two-thirty. Now go back to sleep." She kissed my forehead and then disappeared.

At nine, my phone rang.

"Good morning, baby."

"Hi, Mom!"

"You have a niece!"

"Is she cute?"

"Yes! She is adorable."

"What is her name?"

"Abigail Sara Delecroie Gilmore."

"How long do you think it will take her to learn that one?"

"She is a Delecroie; she will be smart."

"When do we get to see her?"

"This afternoon. They are going to rest for a while."

They came home three days later; Chris would not leave Ann's side. Mom was excited about having Abigail around, but not thrilled about being called Grandma. A week later, Kate and Elizabeth boarded a plane for New York. Lizzy was excited about starting at NYU. Hope and I spent out last week of vacation not worrying about anything—school or careers.

This year was going to be boring for the accelerated program. All book and busy work. We knew we had to get through it and everything would be good. We both had lots of homework every night and at least one report to do over the weekends. The first thing we would do when we got home was see Abigail and then work on our schoolwork.

"Happy birthday, baby."

I opened my eyes and looked up. "Morning, Mom."

"I know it is your birthday; however, you still have to go to school. We will celebrate when you guys get home."

After school, we both ran in and saw Abigail. The Johnsons stopped by; they got Hope and I a gift certificate each to a bookstore. After they left, we had dinner and then the best part: presents! We each received the normal clothes, CDs and DVDs. I received some new soccer things, a new riding outfit, and some law books. Hope had some swimming things, a new riding outfit, and some medical books.

"Are you guys ready for your last gift?"

"Yes, please!"

Mom picked up two envelopes and handed them to us. Inside were certificates for drivers education.

"You're actually going to let us take drivers education?"

"As much as I do not want you to, I do have to let you learn to drive; you are growing up!"

We jumped up and gave them both a hug. On top of our already hectic schedules, we added two days of drivers ed a week. On Sunday mornings, I started sleeping late due to exhaustion.

"Tanya, it is eleven, time to get up."

"What?"

"You have slept away half of the morning, baby. Do I need to send Emily in to take a look at you?"

"No, I am not sick—well, maybe a cold, but that is it."

"Well, it is time to get up. Your sisters are coming in from New York, and they will be here shortly."

"All right."

"Oh, I almost forgot. We are spending this week on the yacht."

"The what?"

"Your father decided that he wanted a new toy. I agreed that we would spend Thanksgiving on it."

"All right. I will be right down."

She turned and looked at me. "I want you to drink two glasses of orange juice with your brunch."

"Okay," I replied, rather than arguing about it. I actually liked orange juice, but I vowed never to tell her that.

Elizabeth, Kate, and William all arrived that afternoon. The next morning, we left for the harbor. The first surprise Dad had for us was the name. He called it *Sara's Star*. Dad was very excited about the boat. It was 150 feet long and had a captain, a cook, a maid, and a butler. Aside from the servants' quarters, there were five bedrooms and a living, dining, and recreation room. The main deck even had a hot tub! The master bedroom had its own bathroom; the other bedrooms had a bathroom connecting two rooms. Hope and I shared one room connecting to Elizabeth's. Abigail's crib went into Ann and Chris's room and then a playpen into the living room. We sailed to Catalina and then on to San Diego.

Thanksgiving dinner was the usual holiday event. When dessert was served, Abigail started crying.

"I will take care of her."

"Thanks, Mom. She is a handful."

"This little angel! She is not going to stay this size forever. It has been so long since the triplets were born that I still miss this size."

"Mom, does that mean you won't mind more grandchildren then?"

"No, Kate, this one got me over being called Grandma; I look forward to having more in the future. Not for a long time from you two," she said, looking over at Hope and me.

"How about May?"

"May?"

"Another grandchild in May."

"Kate Lynn, are you?"

"Yes, I am due May 5th."

The next three days were filled with the talk of a new baby. Mom wanted Kate to move back to California; however, Dad interjected and said that he needed her in New York for the company. They finally agreed that when Kate was about ready, Mom would go to New York City. Hope and I were slated to be out of school about a week later; then Dad would take us out to New

York City where we would spend the summer!

After Thanksgiving break, we started taking our exams for this term. I was not as stressed out as I had been for the last ones. I was already in the program; now I just had to keep up my grades. The final morning of the term, we received our report cards. I received a B+ in English law terminology. All the rest of my grades were A's. I had to maintain an 80% average in all of my classes to remain in the program so I was not worried about that; however, I knew Dad would not be happy.

Ann and Chris were in New York, so it was just the four of us for dinner. The main course was nearing an end; I knew he would want to see our reports.

"Girls, hand them over." I looked at Hope and then slowly got mine out and handed it over to him. He looked it over, then handed it to Mom, who looked at it.

"Tanya, this is not like you. I do not believe that you have ever have gotten a B."

"I know. I am really sorry. I will work harder."

"I have been watching you; I know you are working hard. While you are on vacation, write out all of the things that you had trouble with, and then we will go over them. Next term, if you have any problems, you will ask me for help, agreed?"

"Yes, sir."

"Good, now one more thing. Hand over your learner's permit. NO driving for two weeks."

I had to smile as I pulled it out. This was not really a punishment. The only time I got to drive was home from school; Hope got to drive to school.

"Tanya, the Johnsons called and asked if you two could come over for a Christmas celebration."

"I don't want to go over there on Christmas."

"You are going over on the 23rd for the afternoon. So I think tomorrow we need a shopping trip so you two can buy presents."

The next day, the three of us spent the entire day shopping, and we had lunch on the coast. Hope and I bought Sam a laptop since she was always saying how jealous she was of ours. For Isabelle, we bought her a pink child's computer, and for Liz and Jeff, we bought a certificate for a weekend on the *Queen Mary*. They were thrilled when we gave them their presents two days later. Sam was the happiest.

When we got home, Ann, Chris, Kate, William, and Elizabeth were all home. We talked for a while and then went to bed. Christmas Eve and

Christmas were what I had come to expect from this family. My family. I was given my usual gifts: clothes, soccer things, law books, and then two suits.

"Girls, you are getting older. You are really young women, and there will be some occasions for which you may want to dress more adult."

That was proven a week later when Dad had his associates over for New Years. Hope and I both wore suits instead of our normal pleated skirts and blouses.

"Tanya, Hope, you remember Mr. and Mrs. Camden."

"It is very nice to see you again, Mrs. Camden, Mr. Camden."

"Craig, they have grown up so much even since May. You must be so proud!"

"Yes, I am, and in a few years, Hope will be Dr. Hope Delecroie. And little Tanya will be a new executive at Delecroie Enterprises."

"That is wonderful! They have their futures already planned out! I am just hoping that Arial will stay out of trouble and hopefully graduate."

"How is she doing at the Silvan School?"

"She has been there for six months, and I think she is starting to figure out that we are serious. We told her if she wanted to come home for Christmas she had to get out of the negative on demerits. She did not, and so we left her there. I hope that this tough love is really worth it."

"I am sure it will be. Have you met the newest addition to our family?" he said as Mom walked over carrying Abigail."

"No, she is adorable."

"Yes, she is."

"What is this we heard that you are going to get another one of these?"

"Yes, Kate is due in May. My oldest two have decided to make me a grandmother, and my youngest two are not even allowed to date yet." They all laughed.

When school started, I made sure to get my grade back up; I did not want to see how Dad would react if I did not bring it back up. I had a little more time at first because we were done with drivers training, although I wanted to play soccer again. I knew I had to do something, so I decided to combine them. I would run drills out in the yard while quizzing myself on the terms. I spotted Mom watching me a few times, but she never said anything. I was always showered and dressed for dinner, and when Dad would give me a quiz, I answered everything correctly. Hope and I continued to spend every other Saturday with the Johnsons. On the first of May, Mom left for New York. Two days later, she called and said that we had another niece: Jessica Bree.

Hope and I both took our exams and received all A's. We then joined everyone else in New York City. Mom and Dad split Kate's job responsibilities at the office, and Mom was going to take over temporarily. Emily moved to New York that week also; Mom decided to offer her the job of watching after the babies rather than us. Elizabeth was not happy about everyone being there. She was showing that her normal schedule was being thrown off. Dad reinstated a curfew on her, which she complained about, and was advised that she should be happy that that was the only thing. Hope and I spent the summer shopping and seeing shows, and Mom enrolled us both in a summer program at the Sharp Academy. She did not want us wasting the whole summer. In midsummer, the Johnsons arrived for a vacation. They were staying at the hotel.

"Miss Tanya, Miss Hope, the Johnsons are here to see you."

They came through the door. Sam was looking around. "This is almost as impressive as your house in California."

"Hi, Sam! Let me give you a quick tour, and then we will move onto the city!"

"Where are your parents?" Liz asked.

"They both went into the office today, some meetings. They said we could take the limo."

"That is nice of them."

I opened the door to my room. "This is mine."

"Tanya, this is not fair. You have two very cool rooms."

"You should see the one I have in London."

We concluded the tour and then asked where they wanted to start.

"Mommy, can we go see the stars?"

"Isabelle, we are going to do that in the morning when they have a TV show outside."

"Oh."

"Why don't we start with Ellis Island and the Statue of Liberty, have lunch downtown, then see Times Square and Radio City Music Hall, and conclude with dinner and a show?"

"Sounds good."

Isabelle was asleep by the time we dropped them off at the hotel. Mom was waiting for us when we arrived at home. "Did you two enjoy yourselves?"

"Yes, they really enjoyed it."

"Was Isabelle more excited about the limo or the city?"

"I am not sure." I smiled at her. "Mom, I am tired, and I am going to bed."

"Me, too."

"Good idea. Enjoy your rest!"

"Goodnight, Mom."

We each gave her a hug and retreated to our rooms. When the week was over, Hope and I were both exhausted; we had done everything there was to do in New York City, plus a few extras! We spent the weekend resting and then started a new program at the Sharp Academy on Monday.

Chapter Twenty-Two

By August, Abigail was crawling all over the place and walking as long as she could hold onto something. Jessica was rolling over on her own. Mom was not too pleased when she had to say goodbye and leave Jessica and Kate in New York while we returned to California. Kate had to keep reminding her that it would not even be a month before they came home again. Mom was throwing us a 16th birthday party! There were going to be over 150 people there. All of our friends and several of Dad's associates were also going to attend.

Three days before the party, Mom came into my room. "Hello, Tanya."

I looked up at her from my desk. "Hey, Mom, what's up?"

"Is that the proper English?"

"Hello, Mother. How may I assist you this fine day?"

"All right, smarty. We do need to talk." She sat down on the couch.

I walked over and sat on the table across from her. "About what?"

"There is someone coming to your party."

"Mom, there are a lot of someone's coming to the party."

She smiled at me. "Yes, there are; however, there is one whom you should know about: your Grandmother Megan."

"My grandmother? I have one? I just assumed…I guess I really don't know. I never thought about it."

"I am sorry I have never really said anything about her; it is just that my mother and I don't quite see eye to eye on things, so we rarely speak. She still lives in Australia."

"Why do you not get along?"

"She did not approve of your father; she never forgave me after I married him and moved back to the states. She called today, said that she knew there was a sixteenth birthday party coming up, and that she would be here. I told her when the party was."

"Did you talk to her for a while?"

"No, that was it."

"When is she arriving?"

"I have no idea. I have to go tell Hope." She stood up and kissed the top of my head.

She arrived on Friday. We were having dinner on the patio, and the babies were both off with Emily on a walk.

"Is this how I am welcomed into my own daughter's house, Kerstin?"

We all looked up; Mom stood up quickly. "Mother, I am sorry, we did not know that you were arriving tonight." She walked over and gave her mother a quick hug.

"I told you that I would be here for the party. Oh well. Kate, Ann, Elizabeth, Hope, Sara, come give your grandmother a kiss."

Nobody moved, and then Mom walked behind me. "Mother, I tried to tell you." She put her hands on my shoulders. "This is Tanya, not Sara."

"Tanya? What? When did this happen? Where is Sara?"

"Tanya came back four years ago. I ran into her in a theater. Sara…Two years ago, the triplets were in a very bad car accident. Sara did not survive."

She looked shocked. "You could have called me, Kerstin."

"I tried. I left so many messages for you to call me back, but you never did, so I gave up."

"Pish-posh. Tanya, come here and let me get a look at you."

I looked up at Mom; she smiled at me, then stepped back so I could stand up. I was still wearing my uniform.

"Well, I see that you go to a private school. Very well, although you should be in a finishing school, preferably in England."

"Mother, my daughters are being educated, not finished off to be married."

"Kerstin, hush, I am not speaking to you. Tanya, give me a kiss."

I did and then returned to my seat. Mom started playing with my hair as Grandma Megan inspected the rest of my sisters, then sat down in Mom's spot. Mom remained standing behind me.

"What else have you neglected to tell me, Kerstin?"

"The phone works both ways, Mother."

"Kerstin Alexandra, do not speak to me like that."

"Yes, Mother. Other things that are new. Kate and Ann are both mothers."

"I am a great grandmother? Boys or girls?"

"Girls. Jessica and Abigail. Elizabeth is in her second year of college."

"Girls. I should have known, and I never did see why you waste your money on sending girls to college."

Mom's hands tightened on my shoulders. "Mother, the room that you used before has been transformed into a nursery for Abigail."

"Fine, I will take the room at the end of the triplets' hall."

"Sorry, Mother, that is Emily's room."

"Who is Emily?"

"Our nanny. She was helping take care of Hope and Tanya when they were sick, and now she looks after Abigail and Jessica."

"You gave hired help a room like that? She should be in the servant's area. What room do you have for me to use?"

"The room next to Elizabeth's has been made up for your arrival."

"Fine. Now, why did you hire someone to take care of your children when they were sick? Were you too busy with that company?"

"Mom was with me the whole time."

"Hush, child, I was not speaking to you."

"I was not too busy for them, but they needed more than just me. Hope was temporarily paralyzed in the car accident. As for Tanya, she was diagnosed with leukemia five months after she came home."

"Oh NO."

"She is fine; she has been in remission now for almost two years."

"Good, good."

I looked back up at Mom. "Mom, I told Sam that I would call her."

She looked down at me. "Okay, baby, why don't you and Hope go do that?"

We both stood up. "Thank you."

When we got upstairs, Hope told me what she remembered about the last time Grandma Megan had visited; she and Sara had been only five, though, so it was not much. We remained in my room the rest of the evening.

The next morning, I looked out of my window to see that the yard had been transformed with balloons, tables, and chairs. I put on a white sundress with purple flowers, and white open-toed sandals, which Mom had bought us for that day. I decided to leave my hair down. It now came down to my lower back. I was brushing it out when Hope knocked on my door.

"Are you ready?"

"Yeah, you?"

"Yeah, let's go."

We walked out to the patio. Mom was out there with Grandmother Megan. "Happy birthday, girls!"

"Thanks, Mom."

"You both look so grown up; it seems like just yesterday you were learning how to walk."

"Kerstin, do not get sentimental."

Mom gave us both a hug and ignored her own mother.

The guests started to arrive and so did the presents! There were two tables set up for just those. We decided that we would donate anything that was a duplicate or that we already had. By the time the party was over, the table was overfilled. We opened all of the gifts after the guests departed.

"All right, girls, are you two ready for your last gift from your mother and I?"

Hope and I both smiled. "Yes, Daddy!"

Mom started laughing. "Okay, now close your eyes." We both did. "All right, now open!"

They were both holding a set of keys. Hope and I looked at each other.

"Keys to a car?"

Dad started laughing now. "Yes, Hope, they are out front."

We both jumped, took the keys, and ran toward the front door. There sat a red and a blue sports car, both with a bow on the hood.

"Are you two happy?" Mom asked as she and Dad caught up with us.

"Yes! Thank you!" We gave them both a hug and a kiss, then checked out our new cars.

I was drained when I got back to my room; I changed for bed and then started reading my book. There was a knock on my door.

"Come in." Grandmother Megan appeared. "Grandmother."

"Did you enjoy your party?"

"Yes."

"Good." She stood there for a moment.

"Is there something I can do for you?"

"I do have something I would like to discuss with you."

"All right."

She sat down on the corner of the bed. "Your mother has taken you to England?"

"Yes."

"What about Australia?"

"No."

"I would like you to come home with me. I want to get to know you. We will spend some time together, and you will be back here in no time."

"I know you are my grandmother; however, I do not know you."

"That is why I want you to come. Get to know you."

"What did my parents say?"

"Your mother said that the final decision would be left to you."

"I am not sure. I have school and things to do here."

"I really want to get to know you. I have missed so much with your sisters, and I want a chance at a relationship with at least one of my grandchildren."

"When would we leave?"

"The flight goes in three hours."

"What?"

"Yes, go get changed. I will pack a bag for you."

"I need to go talk to my mom."

"You know that she went out with your father and his associates for a nightcap."

"She would not just let me take off to another country and not come say anything to me."

"I told her I would leave her a note, and then she could meet us at the airport to say goodbye."

I felt really weird about it, but she was so pushy, I agreed to go, but then she would not even let me go say goodbye to Hope, claiming she did not want her to feel really bad. Three hours later, she had me on the airplane. Mom had not shown up. I knew something was wrong, but everything was kind of fuzzy and had been since we had arrived at the airport. I slept the entire flight. Grandmother Megan had slipped me a sleeping pill in a drink she had bought while we had waited for the flight.

She lived in an estate about half the size of the house in England. She showed me to a room. "This is where you will stay. It used to be your mother's room until she ran off with your father."

"I need to call my mom."

The phone started ringing.

"That will be your mother now." She walked over and picked up the phone. "Hello?…Yes, Kerstin, she is here…She really did not have a choice, and you know I am not going to just send her back; you need to come get her…Nope, I locked up her passport; I will only hand it over to you."

I was sitting on the bed; my head was still a little foggy, but I knew what was going on.

"Yes, she is right here, but let me warn you, she may not make a whole lot of sense right now…No, it was just something to make the trip easier for her. Hold on." She handed me the phone.

"I am sorry, Mom."

"It is okay baby; I am going to be on the next flight out there. Are you all right?"

"Yes, fine."

"Good. I am getting onto the plane. I will see you shortly. I love you!"

"Love you too." I hung up the phone and looked up. "You lied to me and drugged me or something."

"Yes, I did, but I need your mother here, and you are a sure way of getting her here."

"Why do you need Mom here?"

"Do not worry about it. Why don't we set all that aside and learn a little about each other?"

She was actually a very interesting person and she took an interest in my education. She was quite happy that mom actually insisted that we get good educations.

"Why do you pretend to be against it then?"

"I do not want your mother to think that I approve of what she has done with her life."

"But if you did, then wouldn't your relationship be a little better?"

"Probably not. We have not gotten along since we moved her here; she never was too fond of Australia. However, it is for our relationship that I want her out here."

"I am tired. I think I want to go to bed."

"You have not eaten anything since you got here."

"That is all right, I am not hungry."

"I am not letting you get sick; then your mother will really kill me. Go change. I will have something sent up to your room."

After I ate, I fell fast asleep. When I woke up, Mom was next to me.

"Morning, baby."

"Hi, Mom."

"Are you ready to go home?"

"Yes. Have you spoken to Grandmother yet?"

"No. I still have my key, and I figured she would put you in here."

"Maybe you should go talk to her."

"I have to go get your passport from her. Baby, whatever you do, never trust your grandmother."

"Trust me, I won't. I am still trying to figure out how I got here."

She kissed the top of my head. "All right, I am off to slay the evil dragon." She stood up and walked toward the door.

I got dressed and headed out toward the dining room.

"That does not give you the right to take my daughter out of the country without my knowledge."

"You are right. I am sorry, but it was the only way I knew I could get you to come here."

"You could have asked me, Mother."

"You would not have come."

"You do not know that."

"Kerstin, you know you would not have come."

"Okay, so I probably would not have come, but you still had no right to take Tanya. What is so important, anyway?"

"It is something I had started before you ran away. I was going to have it released to you after you returned and that boy had ruined your life."

"Mother."

"Let me finish. I was thrilled when you called and said that you had finished college. I figured your relationship had to be almost over; then you were pregnant. I did not want you to end up like me. I knew you wanted to become a success. I did not want you strapped down with having to raise a child."

"I am successful, and I have had six children. I did both."

"Yes, you are quite good at both also. I had that fund set up for you so you would have something when you would come home heartbroken, but you never did. That never happened, and that trust fund had grown quite nicely."

"I am sure it has. Why did you not just take the money out?"

"It was meant for you, although I do want to take it out now. I want to put it into a trust fund for each of the girls."

"They all already have very nice trust funds."

"I am sure they do; however, I do have to do something with my estate, and they are my heirs."

"All right, so why do you need me?"

"We both have to be present at the bank to retrieve the money."

"When can we do that?"

"The day after tomorrow."

Mom sighed, then looked up to see me standing in the door. "Well, Tanya, it looks like we are staying for a few days."

"We can show her where you spent your rebellious years."

I started laughing at that.

"Mother."

"Well, Kerstin, it is the truth"

They did get along the days we were there. They gave me a good tour and showed me where Mom had gone to school, where she had gone to hang out, and where my grandfather had started his business. For lunch, we went into a little diner.

"Megan! Good to see you. Wait, this young one looks like the spitting image of Kerstin."

Mom turned to him. "Mac, it is good to see you again."

He turned to her. "Oh, my, is it really you, Kerstin? She must be yours."

"Yes, she is my youngest. This is Tanya."

"Youngest? You mean there are more of these darlings?"

"Kerstin has six daughters and two granddaughters."

"You are too young to be a grandmother. Wow, six daughters."

"Well, my last three were triplets. As for being a grandmother; you would have to tell my oldest two that."

"Do you have pictures?"

"Of course I do." She opened her purse and retrieved the photos. Grandmother and Mac both looked at them. "Mother, why don't you keep those? I can get more when I get home."

"Thank you, Kerstin."

"Tanya, what do you think of Australia?"

"It is quite different from home."

"Yes, it is. Your mother was crazy for leaving here."

"If she had not, then I would not be here."

"Quite true. She is lovely, Kerstin. She will marry well."

"Not until after she finishes law school and then some."

"Passing your views onto your children? Tanya, you do not want to go to law school, do you?"

"Yes, I quite enjoy it."

"You should come live with your grandmother for a while, and then you could enjoy real things."

"Mac, leave the child alone. They are here for a short visit, and I would appreciate it if you did not scare her into never coming back."

We had dinner back at Grandmother's, and then we sat on the porch and looked out over the grounds. Mom and Grandma talked about stories of when Mom had been little. I fell asleep sitting out there.

"Baby, let's get you upstairs."

"Kerstin, I thought you traveled with the child. She should be used to time changes."

"Mother, just because we adapt to them easily does not mean that she does. She is still in remission, and that means that she is still fragile. And these have been a few big days for her."

"You are right. I am sorry."

"Mother, are you feeling all right?"

"Yes, why?"

"You have apologized to me twice and defended my actions to Mac."

"I would like to rebuild a relationship with my only child."

"That would be nice. I need to get her upstairs, and then I will be back down."

"All right."

Mom slipped her arm around me. "Come, Tanya. Time for bed." In my room, she got out my pajamas, handed them to me, kissed the top of my head, and then left the room. The following day, we did more sightseeing. Mom and Grandmother got along much better; now they seemed like they were actually related. When it was finally time for them to go to the bank, Mom decided that she wanted me to go along as well.

"Welcome, Mrs. Dunn, Mrs. Delecroie, and Miss..."

"Delecroie. This is my granddaughter, Mr. Kidman."

"How nice. I take it she will be joining us?"

"Yes," my mother replied. We went into a large office where there was another man already sitting.

"Ladies, this is Charlie Ingo. He is the lawyer working on the paperwork."

"It is nice to finally meet you, Mrs. Delecroie. Now, shall we get down to business?"

"Yes, please."

"All right. The established trust Mrs. Megan Caitlin Dunn set up for her daughter, Kerstin Alexandra Dunn, now known and Mrs. Kerstin Alexandra Delecroie, is now worth 10 million dollars. As we understand it, Mrs. Dunn, you have suggested that your daughter no longer needs the trust, and you wish to have it divided up amongst Mrs. Delecroie's children?"

"Yes, that is correct."

"Are we going to invest this money into trust funds for your girls?"

Mom looked at Grandmother. "I am not sure what good it would do to put the money into a trust fund; all of the girls already have a 10-million-dollar trust fund. Maybe the money should be invested?"

I could hardly believe what I heard. I had known that I had a trust fund, but I had had no idea it was that much.

"Kerstin, investments would be good, but they are all getting older. Maybe we should just set them up with an account and let them decide what they want to do with it."

"Yes, Mother, I like that idea."

"What are the girls' names and ages?"

"Tanya Alexandra Delecroie, age 16; Hope Victoria Delecroie, age 16; Elizabeth Samantha Delecroie, age 19, Ann Mary Delecroie Gilmore, age 26, and Kate Lynn Delecroie Lord, age 28."

"And the sixth child?"

"She has passed away."

"All right, we will place two million dollars in an account for each of the five names listed. Who should we put down as co-administer?"

Mom and Grandma looked at each other. "Mother, it is a gift from you."

"Kerstin, I gave that money to you 28 years ago. It should be your name."

"Mother, why don't we put my name on Hope's and Tanya's; they are still underage. I will be making the decisions for them right now anyways. Then your name goes with the other three."

Mom and Grandmother both signed several documents, and then they were finally finished. When we got into the car, Grandmother looked at Mom. "I am guessing you will take her and be on the next flight back to California?"

"Yes. Well, she is missing school. She is a junior, and we do not want her to fall too far behind."

"A junior? You mean sophomore."

"No, after the accident, the girls were both home schooled for a term. When they went to their new school, they both tested to be in the second term of ninth grade. They pretty much skipped the eighth grade."

"That is wonderful!" She paused. "Just stay a few more days."

"If we leave now, she can go to school on Friday and spend the weekend catching up. Mother, why don't you spend Christmas with us?"

"Will you be in California or New York?"

"California."

"I will come as long as you promise to spend their summer break here."

"Three months is a long time. Maybe a week or two."

"All right, but you let this one and her sister stay longer."

"I will let them stay longer, but you also have to take Sam."

"Who is this Sam?"

"She is the oldest daughter of the family who had been raising Tanya."

"I am not kidnapping the child just so you can get revenge."

I started laughing.

"No, Mother. Sam, Tanya, and Hope are going to a college prep program together this summer. If I am going to tell Sam that there has been a change in plans, then she is to be included."

"Are her parents really going to let you send their daughter to a foreign country?"

"Sure, as long as we do not tell them that she will be staying with a crazy old lady."

I started laughing again.

"Kerstin, are you trying to teach your child how to disrespect her parents?"

"Sorry, Mother."

Grandmother gave Mom a hug. "All right, get this child back to her school, but remember our deal."

"I will if you do."

"Come here, child."

I gave her a hug.

"I will see you at Christmas, and I guess I should meet this Samantha then, also."

"Do not worry, Mother, you will. I will call you when we get home."

We waved goodbye as the taxi pulled away.

"I guess you and I needed a short vacation."

"Am I grounded?"

"What, for letting your grandmother take you out of the country and not telling me?"

"How long this time?"

"If you ever leave the country again without telling me, it will be until you are married."

"So I am not grounded?"

"You are until we get home."

"Thanks, Mom. Are you and Grandmother really going to mend your relationship?"

"We are going to try. We talked a lot, and I think we understand each other a little better."

"I am glad."

Chapter Twenty-Three

We arrived home late Thursday night. Hope was already in bed, and Dad met us by the front door.

"Tanya, I am glad you are home. This house has been quiet with just Hope here."

I smiled at him, but Mom looked confused. "Just Hope? Where is Ann and Abigail?"

"They went back to New York City with Chris. How was dealing with your mother?"

"Very interesting. She will be joining us for Christmas."

"What?"

"It is a long story. I will tell you upstairs. Tanya, off to bed."

I gave them both a hug and went to my room. All of my presents had been moved in there already including my car keys! I had forgotten all about that!

Hope let me drive to school on Friday since she had gotten to all week long. I told her all about the trip, and how they had shown me where Mom used to hang out, and how Grandma wanted us to come stay with her this summer. She decided that it would be okay after I told her how Mom said that if we were to go then Sam had to go also.

I received my entire week's worth of homework on Friday; it was enough to keep me busy the entire weekend. When I got home, I went straight to work until Mom told me to come down for dinner. I worked all day Saturday and on Sunday, all except for our family brunch. On Monday, Mom surprised me and said I had another checkup. I still hated those. If they said it was back, my whole life would change again; it would all be turned upside down, and now everything was just going great!

The doctor agreed and said I was still good.

When we arrived home, there was a police car sitting at the entrance. Mom and I went inside. Mary met us by the door.

"Mrs. Delecroie, your husband and daughter are in the den. He asked that you both join them as soon as you arrived."

Mom looked down at me; I could see the scared look in her eyes, but she did not say anything. She just took my hand and led the way to the den. Hope was sitting next to Dad on the couch, and there were two detectives sitting across from them. They all looked up as we entered the room.

"Mrs. Delecroie, we are sorry to catch you off guard like this."

She looked from Dad to the detectives. "What is going on?"

"We have in custody the man responsible for your daughter's kidnappings."

"Which time?"

"Both. It was the same person. When he realized what a mistake he had made the first time not using her for ransom, he decided that he would try it again to correct that mistake."

I moved into Mom, and she wrapped her arms around me. "Thank you for letting us know. What do we need to do now?"

"Well, we are building our case, and we would like it if Tanya would be one of our witnesses."

"NO, I will not allow that; she is not being dragged through this again."

"Mom, may I have a say?"

"You are not doing it."

I moved out from her hold, so I was now facing her. "Mom, I know that it will be upsetting, and I know that it will be far from easy; however, what kind of an attorney am I going to make if I cannot even be a witness to a crime committed against me? How is that going to look?"

Dad had gotten up and was behind me. He laid a hand on my shoulder. "She has a point, Kerstin." She looked at both of us. "Why, out of six children, does this one have to be the stubborn one?"

"Mom, we have already concluded that I get that from you," I said and smiled at her.

She started laughing. "All right, fine. However, if at any time she is in any danger, she is out of there."

"Yes, ma'am, the last thing we would want is to put her in any more danger. We will have the prosecutor contact you to speak to Tanya."

We went out to dinner to celebrate this guy finally being caught. Three weeks later, the prosecutor wanted to see me. We went over every detail of the second kidnapping. And also over some of the details of the first, such as how scared I had been. Since I was too young to remember the first time, they wanted to know the details of finding out about being kidnapped, and how I felt when I was returned to my family of strangers. The meeting lasted about two hours; Dad was with me the whole time. Then afterward he took me out for ice cream.

"Tanya, I want to make sure you understand that when this trial starts, your picture is going to get plastered on every newspaper and magazine again."

"Because I am testifying?"

"No, because you are Tanya Alexandra Delecroie, heir to Delecroie International and the Delecroie fortune. You were kidnapped not once, but twice, and everyone will be interested."

"I figured as much. They said the trial would be in February. So it will only be a few months. If the media does not die down by the time school is out, I will go to Australia a month early."

"Your mother won't like that, but you are right, it will be the best plan. You will be a household name."

"Dad, I really do understand."

"Good."

Grandmother arrived three days before Christmas; the house was back to being full of people. Dad barely said anything to her; however, she never said one negative thing about him or how he raised his children. The Johnsons spent Christmas Eve with us; Sam was excited to meet Grandmother and even more excited that she would be spending the summer with us in Australia. Christmas was good. Grandmother left two days after, and everyone else left two days after New Years.

The days until the trial seemed to fly by. The week before the trial, I met with the lawyers one more time. The trial went pretty fast; there was a lot of evidence against this guy. It lasted about two and a half weeks, ending at the beginning of March. Dad was right. My picture was in every magazine and paper. Every time I turned on the news, it was about me. Three days after the trial ended, Mom picked me up during school.

"The verdict is in," she told me.

We went to the courthouse. Dad met us there inside. The man was found guilty, along with the two who had to help him. They were all sentenced to 120 years in prison with no chance of parole.

A month later, I was still popular. Everyone wanted to meet me. Mom decided Dad was right. They decided to send me to Australia as soon as school was finished in three weeks. They also decided that Hope would wait until Sam was out of school, so the two of them would join me three weeks after I had gotten there. The night before I left, Hope and I stayed up in my room.

"This is longer than we have been away form each other in the last four years."

"I know. I wanted to go, but Mom said that I should wait until Sam is ready, but you have to go."

"They are trying to make us adjust to not being together all the time."

"Why?"

"You are going to med school, I am going to law school, and how many places have both?"

"That is not for another year."

"Yes, but Mom knows she cannot wait til next year before she makes us split up and say, 'You over there, you there, and you will see each other in four months.'"

"Yeah, that would not be good."

"Next, we will be going on separate weekend trips and things."

"What schools have you applied to?"

"I have no idea; I am sure only the best. We will have to look into that when we get home."

We both fell asleep on my bed, and then we had breakfast in my room also.

"Tanya, are you ready?"

"Yes, Mom." I gave Hope a big hug. "I will see you in a few weeks." Mom then gave her a hug, and we left.

We arrived at Grandmother's in mid afternoon. Mom stayed for two days and then returned to California. Grandmother and I got along for the first few days, and then it started to fall apart.

"Tanya, why don't we enroll you in school?"

"Grandmother, I am on summer vacation."

"Yes, but you should know how other places operate."

"Grandmother, why do you never go to New York City?"

"I do not like big cities. But I am not sure what…"

"You should know how other places work."

"You, child, are exactly like your mother."

"Thank you."

"I mean stubborn and defiant."

"Yes, she is already aware of that. Not too happy, although she deals."

"Why don't you just go find something to go do?"

I started walking away. When I got to the door, I looked back over my shoulder. "The bar is on the main road, right?" I asked and kept walking.

"Tanya Alexandra, you better not."

I was not sure what it was about this place; I just felt the need to be free! It brought out my rebellious side. I stayed out late, slept in late, and hung out with a group of guys I met in town. I lost track of time and forgot what day Mom was bringing Hope and Sam.

When I got back to my room at 1 a.m. and turned on my light, I froze. My mother had been sitting in the dark waiting for me. "Uh, Mom."

"Uh, Tanya. What do you think you are doing, young lady?"

"I, umm."

"Your grandmother said that you have been acting like this since I left."

"Well…"

"I want to know what excuse you have?"

"I do not know. She just kept saying that I was exactly like you, and I am not sure what came over me. I was having real fun. I am sorry."

"You should be. I should take you home with me tomorrow."

"Please let me stay."

"You are apologizing to your grandmother first thing in the morning, and then you will change back into the well-behaved daughter I am used to having around."

"Yes, Mother."

"Good. Now go change. I am staying in here tonight. No need to set up another room for one night when that night is almost over."

I crawled into bed and fell asleep. However, I did not sleep in in the morning.

"Wake up, young lady. You have some things to go take care of. Your grandmother is on the porch."

I picked up an outfit I had altered since I had come there. She looked at it, then at me. "I do not think so." She went over and opened the closet. "Young lady, you have ruined half of your wardrobe."

"I am sorry."

"You will be paying for the replacements."

"Yes, ma'am."

She took out an outfit—knee-length skirt, white blouse, and knee-high socks.

"Button the shirt all the way up."

I did and then put on a headband and my shoes.

"Now that is what a respectable 16-year-old should be wearing. You are so lucky that your father is not here."

"Yes, ma'am." I walked down to the porch. Mom was behind me, but she stayed out of sight as I made my apology. "Grandmother, I am sorry for how I have been acting. It was rude and shameful of me."

"Thank you. Kerstin, you can come in now."

"Mother, if she starts acting up again, please call me, and she will be on a one-way flight to her father."

Mom gave me the look of "do not try and test me;" she was serious. "Truth be told, Kerstin, she is acting the same way you did when you were her age."

"That is still no excuse."

"No, I am not saying that it is. At least she has not brought home a boy that she says she is going to marry."

"IF she had, she would be locked in her room until she is twenty-five."

"Oh, so you do not approve either?"

"Mother, I am sorry. I never thought of it like that."

"Apology accepted. I will let you know as soon as she shows up with a boyfriend."

"She is too young for a boyfriend."

"She is still standing right here."

"You are not ready for a boyfriend."

"I am sixteen, the age that you and Dad set."

"Well, young lady, after this little stunt, I am not sure how old you have to be now."

"You pulled the same stunt and were married less than two years later."

"That was a different time."

"It still happened."

"Young lady, we are not discussing me. Now go sit on the sofa on the veranda; we both need a cooling-off time. I will come speak to you soon."

I left the room but hid behind the door.

"Kerstin, she is just trying to find herself. Calm down."

"Find herself? Mother, she knows who she is."

"She could be doing a lot worse things. She has not had an easy life; she has been pretty good about it."

"I know. It is just that none of the other girls have ever acted this way. Elizabeth snuck out once, but that was it."

"Kerstin, the child was kidnapped, returned years later to a family of strangers, diagnosed with leukemia, went into remission, was in a car accident that killed her identical sister, leukemia returned, then remission again, then she was kidnapped again, and now with all of the trial things, I would say that you have been lucky she has taken everything so well."

"I know she has never wanted to speak with a professional or anything."

"Well, why don't we let her have control of her own life to a point this summer, see if we can get her through this?"

"All right."

There was a pause, so I quickly went to the veranda and sat on the couch. Mom followed a few moments later.

"Okay, we need to talk."

"We have been doing that since you got here."

"We need to get to the bottom of this."

"Of what?"

"Of why you are acting out so much. You are not the same child I dropped off here three weeks ago."

"First, I am not a child anymore, and second, I have already told you I do not know why."

"None of your sisters ever went through a stage like this."

"I am not my sisters. I am not Kate, Ann, or Elizabeth, and I am not even Hope or Sara."

"You are right; you are not them. So, Tanya, tell me what it is that you want? What are you thinking about?"

"I want to have fun! Real fun! Not to worry about anything, to have my own style. I do not want to be 'Tanya Alexandra Delecroie, youngest and most watched heir to the Delecroie Empire.' I just want to be Tanya. I can do that here; no one knows me or my past. Mom, please, just remember when you were my age, you wanted to have fun, right?"

She was quiet, just staring at me, and then she put her hand on my knee.

"No drugs, no alcohol, and no sex. Be home by 11 p.m. unless otherwise stated by your grandmother. We will go shopping this afternoon for some new clothes, but nothing provocative."

I was stunned. Was she really saying all of these things? "Are you teasing me?"

"If you are caught with any of the things I said no to, I will turn you over to your father. However, I do agree that you need your space to be yourself this summer. Do you agree to my terms?"

"Yes! Thank you!" I jumped up and gave her a hug.

"Now this is my daughter I was looking forward to seeing," she said, hugging me back.

"I take it you two have come to terms?"

"Yes, Mother. Is an 11 p.m. curfew all right with you?"

"Yes, that is fine, and it goes for all three?"

"Yes, unless you say otherwise."

"Mom, where are Hope and Sam?"

"They are in their rooms sleeping. Why don't you go tell them to get up? We are going shopping!"

Chapter Twenty-Four

Mom was true to her word; she let us each pick out our own clothes. Hope and I still picked out a lot of similar things. We each got jeans and jean shorts, tee shirts, and tank tops.

"Girls, remember that when you come home, these clothes don't. I can blame the pictures on your grandmother."

"Thank you, Kerstin. I do believe that your husband and I will never get along."

We all started laughing. Mom did say that we looked good in these clothes. She left for England that night. I showed Hope and Sam around and introduced them to my friends. They agreed that the town was not much. After two weeks, Sam left; she had to be back for her college entrance exams. Hope and I had two weeks left until Mom would be back to get us. Grandmother decided that we needed to see more of the countryside, so she took us on the train. We concluded the trip with a three-day stay in Sydney! By the time we got back, Mom was already there.

"Kerstin, you are early."

"I know. I missed my girls, so I thought I would come surprise you, but there was no one here," she said, giving us a hug.

"I took the girls to see the country."

"Did you guys have fun?"

"YES, we had lots of fun!"

"Good."

"When are we leaving?"

"Tanya, I told your father we would meet him in New York City on Monday."

"So we get to stay the week?"

"Yes."

"Good. I want to spend time with my daughter too, especially after putting up with this handful!" Mom stared right at me. "She did not clean up her act?"

Grandmother started laughing. "No, Kerstin, they were fine, kept their curfew, and did everything they were asked. Only they have so much energy, how do you keep up with them?"

Now Mom started laughing. "Experience. Really, Mother, is there anything I need to know?"

"Well, I am sure the girls are ready to go see Jonathan and Joshua."

"Girls, whom is your Grandmother talking about?"

Hope and I looked at each other. "Umm."

"Oh, Kerstin, you should see them together; they are all very cute. They are 16-year-old twin boys from town."

"Are they deserving of my daughters?"

"They sure are trying to be."

"And when do I get to meet the boys that have my daughters all excited?"

"Mom."

"It is my job, as your mother, to give you a hard time."

"May we please go? We told them we would come over as soon as we got back."

"No. I have not really seen you all summer; you may, however, ask them to come over here."

They came right over; Mom was very impressed. "So, boys, when is your birthday?"

"August 30th, ma'am."

"And who is older?"

"Josh is by seven minutes."

"Interesting. Hope is older than Tanya by seven minutes. Who is dating whom?"

"Well, Mrs. Delecroie, Hope is seeing Jon, and I am seeing your lovely daughter Tanya."

By the time the week was nearing an end, Mom was ready to go. She went through my wardrobe and decided what I would now need. She deducted $700 from my summer allowance to replace my outfits. On Saturday night, they let us stay out until midnight with Jon and Josh. Grandmother promised to come back to California. She also said that she was going to get a computer so we could email.

We arrived in New York on Monday afternoon. Dad was at the penthouse when we arrived. He gave Mom a hug and then turned toward us. "Welcome home, girls. Did you have fun with your grandmother?"

"Yes!"

"Tanya, come here. I have not seen you in over two months."

"Has it been that long?" I said sarcastically.

"Very funny, child."

"Craig, they are not children anymore, and we are going to have to accept that."

"I know. Girls, I received your acceptance letters today. Would you like to know where you will be attending college?"

"Dad, I was thinking. College is not really for me. I am just not going to go."

"Tanya Alexandra Delecroie."

"Craig, she is joking."

"All right. Hope, you are going to attend an Ivy League medical school. Tanya, you will be attending the same Ivy League law school. And you will be going."

"Yes, sir," I said and gave a little salute. I guess it was a little too sarcastic.

"Young lady, your grandmother may have let you get away with that attitude, but I will not. Do you understand?"

"I did not mean anything."

His look went from mad to madder. Mom jumped in.

"Tanya, room. Craig, why don't we step into the office?"

I quickly turned and went to my room. Hope was right behind me.

"What did you do before I got to Australia?"

"What does that have to do with anything?"

"It may explain what that was about. You know that Dad won't stand for answers like that."

"I know, I was not thinking." I turned and faced her. "And for your info,

I broke every rule, stayed out late, had a lot of fun, and I revamped my wardrobe a bit."

"That would explain why Mom just ordered you all of those new outfits."

"Yeah, however, she took it out of my allowance."

"Hope, please excuse your sister and I."

Hope slipped out of the room quickly.

"What was that about?"

"Why do I have to go back to miss perfection just because we are back here?"

"I never said that you had to; however, that scene was just disrespectful to your father."

"He is trying to control my life!"

"Do you want to go into law?"

"Yes."

"Would you like to attend law school?"

"Yes."

"Then tell me, what is so upsetting?"

"He never asked, just told me that I would be going, that I have no choice."

"Are we going to get this attitude every time we make a decision in your life?"

"I do not know."

"I do. That answer is NO. I covered for you before and I warned you that I would not cover for you again."

"Yes, but you also said that I needed room to be my own person."

"Yes, but not with an attitude."

"I do not have an attitude."

"Yes, you do. As much as I hate to say it, I can no longer baby you. I have always let you get away with things, and you know it."

"I told him I did not mean anything."

"Yes, however, your posture and the rolling of your eyes said otherwise. Those little things show your attitude just as much as your verbal words. Now if you want more control, then you need to drop the attitude and show us a little more respect. This has gone on now for a year, and now it is over. Understand?"

"Yes."

"Yes, what?"

"Yes, Mother, I do understand."

"Good. You are grounded to the apartment until next Monday. If the attitude does not go away by then, you can say goodbye to your phone and freedom for a lot longer."

"Yes, ma'am."

"If you straighten up, maybe next week we will go shopping for some new clothes." She smiled at me. I knew that she still felt guilty whenever she yelled at me. I just had to learn how to use that to my advantage. She left my room and told me to get ready for dinner.

I picked out an outfit, put on a blouse, and left the last two buttons undone. Then I put on a pair of open-toed sandals and left my hair down. When I walked into the dining room, everyone was already seated. I slipped into my chair, not saying anything.

Dad got up and walked over to me. "Stand up." I did as he asked and looked at him, making sure the chair was between us. Without saying anything, he reached over and buttoned the top two on my blouse. "When you show some respect to your mother and myself, then I will respect your decision on how to wear your clothes. Until then, you do as I say."

"Yes, sir," I said and then took my seat again.

Kate looked over at me and started smiling. "Tanya, Mom told me how much fun you had in Australia."

"Yes, I did enjoy myself. Where is Jessica?"

"Asleep in the den. Mom, may Tanya come down to my place after dinner?"

"She is grounded to the apartment."

"Please? I would really enjoy spending some time with my youngest sister."

"All right, but downstairs is the farthest she goes."

When supper was over, Kate really did not give me a choice, so I went down with her. "Tanya, have a seat."

"I do not need another lecture."

"Well, I am hoping that you will tell me what is really up with you."

"Nothing, I am just trying to be me."

"I know you are smart. You are smarter than you are acting. Dad is about compromise. Why are you not using that to your advantage? It works better than being a rebellious teenager."

"Why should I not be the rebellious one? No one else has done it; they have had it easy."

"Do you really want to be a lawyer? Truthfully."

"Yes, I do."

"Do you want to go to law school?"

"I guess."

"NOT good enough. Either you do or you don't."

"I do. It is a great school."

"Correct, it is. I attended there and so did Dad. You do realize that you are supposed to be starting there in just one year?"

"Yes."

"You have received an early acceptance."

"Yes, what is the point, Kate?"

"My point is you have been granted early acceptance; however, it can be rescinded. Acceptance is not just based on education, but also on attitude and appreciation. If their reps showed up here and saw how disrespectful you have been, you would not be attending."

"Because of how I am acting in my own home? Come on."

"How many 16-year-olds do you know who have been accepted into a program most people are 21 or 22 before starting?"

"None."

"And you do not think that this law school is going to keep an eye on you?"

"I guess."

"DO you want to lose your spot?"

"No."

"Then use your brain. You want to keep your spot and you want your independence, so compromise. Dad wants respect; Mom wants to see you happy. She hates seeing you even frown. Remember when you wanted to play soccer, you let Dad help you on your homework that you could have done faster yourself?"

"Yes."

"You got to play soccer. If you want to be independent, then you need show Dad you respect his choices and ideas."

"But then he is still running my life."

"You respect his ways; however, you tactfully introduce your own ideas. Your outfit looked fine the way you had it. Dad would have never said anything if you had not upset him already."

"So I go apologize, make them think they are getting what they want, and then I throw in my ideas"

"You are still young; I forgive you for not yet being a master of manipulation." We both started laughing. "So, Mom said Grandmother was really afraid that you were going to repeat Mom's actions."

"Yes, but I had fun!"

"You would, little sister. You are their youngest, the baby. They may be hard on you, but you have it easy."

"What was it like being the oldest?"

"Well, my teenage years started off difficultly since my baby sister went and got herself kidnapped."

"Yeah, I planned that."

"I got to be guarded everywhere I went. I was thrilled to be at school."

"Kate?"

"Yes?"

"Thank you."

"You are welcome. I know that, at times, you want to talk to someone older than Hope, but there are those things that you just cannot talk to Mom about. I am always here for you."

"Thanks. I should probably get back upstairs."

"Yes, you should."

I walked back upstairs.

Mom, Dad, and Hope were in the living room, playing a board game.

"Dad, Mom, Hope, I want to apologize for how I have been acting. I have been rude and disrespectful. I am very sorry."

Mom and Dad looked at each other. "What did your sister say to you?"

"Let's just say that she made me see the error of my ways."

"Well, good. Apology accepted. Would you like to join us?"

"Yes, I would."

We played for a while that evening. That week, I attempted to do what Kate had said. And it did seem to work. The following Monday, I wore the same outfit I had the last Monday. I left the same two buttons undone. Dad did not say a thing. Mom did take Hope and I shopping, to dinner, and then a show on Tuesday.

Chapter Twenty-Five

On our first day back to school, we were being advised on where our internships would take place. The nine of us met in our normal homeroom.

"You will meet here every morning, then have two hours of general studies. Then each of you will spend the remaining part of the day at your assigned internship. Any questions?"

Everyone was silent. They started with the medical program; Hope was assigned at the national Children's Hospital.

"Next is the law program. Tanya Delecroie, you are at Delecroie International."

"What? That cannot be. Is there not some rule against that?"

"Sorry, in order to be fair to everyone, this is done randomly. Your name was drawn with theirs. You will be reporting to Mr. Delecroie."

She continued with everyone's assignments, and then we left to begin our first day at the internships. I walked into the building and took the elevator to the top floor where Mom and Dad split their offices and a conference room.

"Tanya, are you not supposed to be in school? Who do you want to see? Your mother…"

"Maggie, hi. I am actually here on official business to see Mr. Delecroie."

"Go on in then."

"Thank you." I walked over and knocked on the door.

"Come in." I opened the door and entered. "Tanya, what are you doing here, young lady? Please tell me that you did not get yourself suspended."

"No, sir. I am your new intern for the legal department."

"What? I specifically asked them to put you somewhere else. You are going to work here soon enough; you should get the experience elsewhere."

"She said it was done randomly to make it fair for everyone."

He closed the folder on his desk. "Have a seat. I will see what I can do." He was on the phone for a while and then hung up and looked back at me. "I am sorry, Tanya. It looks like you and I are stuck with each other. So you will get to know the business sooner than planned."

The door opened and Mom stepped in. "Craig, Maggie told me that Tanya was here. What is wrong?" she said and then walked over and put her hand on my shoulder.

"Nothing. There was a mixup, and Tanya is our intern this year."

"What? I thought you asked."

"I did; however, it cannot be changed now."

"Well, you cannot send her to work in the mailroom; she will be the boss of many of these people in a few years."

"I know. Tanya, each year we alternate between having a legal intern and a business intern. We normally have them spend their first few weeks working in the different areas so they know how things really work."

"I do not want to be treated differently."

"I know, and that is why we requested that you be placed elsewhere. Here you are different, and they all know it."

"Craig, what are we going to do?"

"Kerstin, I do not think you need to hire that legal assistant anymore. She can easily deal with that."

"Good idea."

"Tanya, every day you will report to your mother; she will advise you of your tasks for the day."

"Yes, sir."

"Good. Now that we have that settled, I am hungry. Let's have lunch and then get you settled in."

"Lunch does sound good. However, my father forgot to give us our lunch money today. I gave my extra cash to my sister so she could get her lunch."

He looked at Mom. "Oh my, I did forget to give them money today. Well,

I guess that your boss will buy today."

Mom pretty much had me doing research for her. Hope was enjoying her time with the kids and decided that she want to be a pediatrician. I did get to know a lot about Delecroie International, and it was quite interesting, However, working and living with my parents was getting to be a bit much. They knew my every move. I made excuses to get away. I would go see the Johnsons or to a friend's house every weekend. When I did get away, I would drive slowly and take as many back roads as I could.

Grandmother surprised us and arrived for Thanksgiving.

"Tanya, I just sent your car in for a tune-up. Please go home with your mother."

"All right."

Hope followed us in the gates, and Grandmother met us at the door. "Hello, Kerstin, girls. I have just been catching up with Ann and little Abigail. She is getting so big." Mom gave her a hug.

"Hello mother, she is and so is Jessica."

Hope and I both gave Grandmother a hug also.

"This is a surprise."

"Yes, well, I wanted to spend some time with my daughter and all of her children."

We were in the living room when Dad got home. He was not too thrilled to see Grandmother.

"Megan, we were not aware that you were coming here," he said, walking in. He took a seat next to Mom.

"Well, Craig, I just wanted to surprise Kerstin."

"That was nice of you," he said and picked up Mom's hand. "Kerstin was saying that she would like to see you again."

Grandmother looked him over, then turned to us. "How are your internships going?"

"Good. Hope talks nonstop about the kids; my boss is a little strict, though."

"Tanya, where are you interning?"

"Delecroie International."

She looked at me. "Really? How odd. Which one do you report to?"

"Her," I said, pointing at Mom.

"Well, I may be able to help you out there. Kerstin, ease up on your daughter."

"She has it very easy," Mom said, staring at me. I smiled at her.

"Girls, are you coming out to Australia again this summer?"

"Megan, I was meaning to speak to you. I saw the outfits you were allowing the girls to wear while they were there. I do not approve of such clothing."

Grandmother smiled and looked at Mom. "Well, Craig, I decided that although their outfits were very nice and fitting of who they are, they needed to be able to wear something that said 'down under' a little more to let them get the full experience."

"I do appreciate that you kept those clothes there."

"You are welcome."

She stayed through the end of the week. When she was getting ready to leave, she asked me again. "Tanya, you are retuning to stay with me again this summer, correct?"

"Mother, I am not sure that the girls will have time to. They will be getting ready for college."

"Kerstin, I am sure they can spare two weeks."

"Mother, we will see."

I watched the car pull away, then returned to my room and started reading.

"Tanya?" Dad was in the door.

"Yes?"

"Tomorrow, I want you to wear your navy suit, and have your mother French braid your hair."

"Why?"

"Because I said so."

"Sorry. May I ask what occasion is prompting such a request?"

"A representative from the board of education will be by the office tomorrow; I want you to look professional."

"Yes, sir."

The next afternoon, Mr. Jones arrived to meet with Dad. I was in his office when he arrived.

"Please come in, Mr. Jones."

"Thank you, Mr. Delecroie. Please call me Edward."

"Edward, please call me Craig. Have a seat. May I offer you anything to drink?"

"No. Thank you, I am fine."

"Edward, may I introduce you to my youngest daughter? Tanya Alexandra Delecroie."

"Nice to meet you, Mr. Jones."

"Nice to meet you also, Tanya. Should you not be in school preparing for your entrance into law school in the fall?"

"Sir, I am an intern here as part of my education."

"I see. How is it that you ended up at your father's corporation?"

"To be fair to all students, it is done like a lottery. My name was drawn with that of Delecroie International."

"How interesting. Works well for you, Craig."

"Actually, I was hoping that she would be placed elsewhere to gain knowledge of how other places operate. However, she has been wonderful to have around."

"Yes, I am sure. Now down to the purpose of this meeting."

"Yes. Tanya, will you please draft the lease for the Helmet Corporation? You know what property they wanted, correct?"

"Yes, sir."

"Good. When you are finished, you may call it a day. Oh yes, off the record, your mother would like to see you."

"Yes, sir." I turned back to Mr. Jones. "Nice to meet you, Mr. Jones."

"You also, Tanya." I turned to leave. "What a delightful girl. Is her sister the same way?"

"Yes."

I knocked on Mom's door.

"Come in."

I opened the door and stepped in. "Dad said that you wanted to see me?"

"Yes, baby, I forgot about it. You have a checkup at 4:30 p.m."

"Another one? Why?"

"Six months since your last one. If this one goes well, you will have been in remission for three years."

"Then I can quit going?"

"Five years in remission, and then you do not have to go."

"All right."

"I have an appointment. Can I trust you to go alone or should I reschedule?"

"I will be fine, promise."

"Okay. Call me as soon as it is over."

"Okay."

She put her arm around me. "I love you, baby."

"Love you too, Mom."

"Good, now get going."

"Tanya, where is your mother?" the doctor asked when I arrived.

"She had an appointment. I am here by myself."

"All right, let's get started." He drew my blood, and we went through the normal routine of these exams. Then he told me to wait in his office. He joined me about thirty minutes later.

"You said your mother was in a meeting?"

"Yes."

"I think we should call her."

"No, doctor, just tell me."

"I really think we should have one of your parents here."

"You have known me since this all started. Do you think my Mother would have let me come on my own if I could not handle, on my own, what the results are? Please, doctor, just tell me what is going on. Is the leukemia back?"

"No, it is not back yet."

"What does that mean?"

"Your cell count is low, too low. The leukemia has not taken back over yet, but it is getting ready to. We need to do something now."

"What are you saying?"

"If we do not act now and put you on a treatment, then you will be out of remission with in a few weeks."

"What are we going to do?"

"Put you back on medication. Lots of rest. I want you back here in two weeks."

"All right."

"I am going to call your mother."

"No, let me talk to her when I get home. I will tell her to call you if she has any questions."

When I left, I did not call Mom; I did not go home. I drove around for a while. My phone rang, but I ignored it. I lost track of time. I finally found myself sitting in my car outside of the gates. Then I eventually drove up and got out of my car. Mom and Dad were standing on the front steps.

"Tanya Alexandra, where have you been?"

"Driving?"

"Do you know what time it is? You scared your mother to death."

"I am sorry."

"You have been driving around for four hours, and you do not know where you have been?"

"Four hours. No, I am sorry. I do not."

"Craig, something is wrong."

He seemed to ignore her.

"Tanya, inside. Go to your room."

"Yes, sir." I turned and started walking.

"Something is wrong; she is not herself. I should have gone with her to that appointment."

I put my book bag down and sat on the edge of my bed. I am not sure how long I sat there before Mom sat down next to me. "Baby, I know something is wrong. What did the doctor say? Is the leukemia back?"

"No, not yet."

"What is it then?"

"He said that it probably would be within the next few weeks. He put me back on medication to try and avoid that."

She put her arm around me. "Oh, baby. What else did he say?"

"Nothing."

"I am going to call him tomorrow."

"Rest, plenty of rest."

"All right, we will make sure you get it. Now have you eaten?"

"No."

She walked over and ordered me dinner, then sat back down next to me. I lay down and put my head in her lap. She started playing with my hair.

I started crying. "Why?"

"Baby, I am not sure, but we will do what we can to make sure it does not come back."

"How?"

"By doing everything the doctor says."

"Even then you cannot make any guarantees."

"No, baby, I cannot, but you let me worry about that."

"I cannot let you worry about it forever; I am almost an adult."

"Adult or not, you will always be my baby. You can let me worry about it. Remember our deal?"

"What deal?"

"You worry about school and friends; I worry about the medical stuff."

"Oh, yeah."

"Do not worry. Just rest."

I closed my eyes and we sat there.

"Kerstin?"

"Shh, I think she is finally asleep."

"What are we going to do?"

"Anything we have to. He put her back on medication."

"Is it going to work?"

"I hope so."

"I calmed Hope down; she is now in bed."

"Good. Will you call down and cancel her dinner? I do not want to wake her."

"She is upset?"

"It has been over a year since she has curled up like this for me to hold her."

"Why don't we go and let her sleep?"

"I want to hold her for a bit longer; I will meet up with you in a while."

I do not know what happened next; I fell asleep for real. When I woke up, there was a fruit tray next to me with a note. *Baby, rest and do not even think of going to school. I will be home for lunch.*

I spent the morning watching TV and playing on my computer. Mom kept her word and was home by lunchtime. The next day, she let me rejoin my school activities, although they were sending me home early.

One month later was the Christmas holiday. Watching Abigail and Jessica did distract me. Hope and I were inseparable during the holiday. The following day, I was back at the doctor's. It was good news. My cell count was rising! I was out of risk, but he wanted to keep me on the medication.

One week later, Dad hosted a New Years party. Kate and Ann were both spending it with their in-laws. Elizabeth convinced Dad to let her stay in New York, so Hope and I were on our own. I knew several of the guests from the office. Hope and I spent the evening trying to avoid the party. When the clock struck Midnight, everyone toasted.

"Happy New Year, Hope! Tanya."

"Happy New Year, Mom! May we go to bed? I am tired."

"Yes. Go say goodnight to your father." She gave us both a kiss.

When we returned to school, our general studies class turned into a graduation preparation class. At least two days a week, we were doing something to get ready. By the time spring break rolled around, everything was coming along. Mom decided to take us on one last spring break for our childhood. We ended up going to Cancun! When spring break was over, we had just a month left of school. For the last week of school, we ended our internships and joined the rest of the senior class. We had assemblies and meetings all week.

On the day of our graduation, we did not have to report until 11:00 a.m. Mom had breakfast with us. When we arrived at school, we changed into our gowns. Hope and I each received a sash for the National Honor Society, a gold cord for being a 4.0 student, and then a navy cord for the advanced program. The ceremony was scheduled to start at 5 p.m. Hope and I played cards until we were called to join the line and receive our diplomas.

"Hope Victoria Delecroie, National Honor Society, also in the Premier honors program. She is walking with Tanya Alexandra Delecroie, National Honor Society, also in the Premier honors program. The Delecroie sisters have both received early admission for the fall term to a medical and law school, respectively."

When the ceremony was over, we met everyone outside.

"My babies have graduated. Congratulations, girls."

"Thanks, Mom!"

"Now, my girls, are you prepared for the next four years?"

"Craig, just tell them congratulations."

"Grandmother!"

"Congratulations, girls!"

Printed in the United States
48216LVS00004B/187

9 781413 789621